Hawthorne's Odyssey

GHOST STORIES AND
TALES OF THE BIZARRE

GIOVANNI ALABISO

I hope these Tales Really make you ascared!!!

Gianni

ARCHWAY
PUBLISHING

Archway Publishing books may be ordered through booksellers or by contacting:

Archway Publishing
1663 Liberty Drive
Bloomington, IN 47403
www.archwaypublishing.com
844-669-3957

Interior Image Credit: Amber J. Mercer-Emslie

ISBN: 978-1-6657-8247-0 (sc)
ISBN: 978-1-6657-8248-7 (e)

Library of Congress Control Number: 2025916677

Print information available on the last page.

Archway Publishing rev. date: 09/03/2025

HAWTHORNE'S ODYSSEY

CONTENTS

DEDICATION

This book is dedicated to my parents, Charles and Mary, who were involved in some of these stories as well as my Aunt Angie (my mom's sister) who told me a ghost story. And, of course, my dog Teddy Green, who is his own ghost story.

PREFACE

This book has arguably been in the making for over 50 years. Some of the stories in this book are from my childhood and have been told in our family for years. It will be clearly evident which stories are from my childhood.

Many other stories have influences of the history of Salem, Massachusetts. A main influence is the 1692 Salem Witchcraft Trials that has inspired so many. Nathaniel Hawthorne, author of The Scarlet Letter and The House of the Seven Gables, has been another influence and the cover story is about him. He was such an interesting, pensive and brooding soul.

Other influences include television shows and movies about ghosts and various paranormal phenomena. I grew up watching Scooby Doo and was only scared by one episode. The Twilight Zone developed my imagination and made me rethink the ordinary. The X-Files brought that to the next level with stories of the super paranormal. The stories are a pleasing mixture of all of these influences.

Ironically, the cover story, Hawthorne's Odyssey, was written on July 4, 2024 that happens to be the 220th anniversary of Nathaniel's birthday. In addition, some of this book was written while I sat in the backyard of The House of the Seven Gables with a view of Salem Harbor.

I have seen many strange things having worked in a city known for its hauntings. I have had some first-hand experiences and have seen inexplicable anomalies and heard outrageous tales. All of this has contributed to my bizarre imagination that has poured out onto the following pages.

Not every story is about death and ghosts. Some will be endearing and some may actually make you shed a tear or two. Not all ghost stories are scary. Some are profound and uplifting. And yet others will make your heart pound.

Be sure to read this book late at night when you are home alone with rumbles of thunder and flashes of lightning. It would be even better if you were an an old Victorian Mansion.

Enjoy!

HAWTHORNE'S ODYSSEY

A young boy trapses through the heavily wooded area around his new home in Maine.

He walks a few feet, cranes his neck back to look up and marvels at the trees stretching toward the heavens. There's so many of them. It is nothing like he has seen before. He looks straight up as far as he can, nearly falling backwards.

The trees all seem to point to the sun high overhead in the sky above. He walks on through the dense woods mesmerized by nature. He notices small animals, suddenly aware of him, running away. He picks up a stick to use to clear a path ahead of him.

Nathaniel doesn't know what to make of his new surroundings but is eager to explore. The woods are wild and primeval to him.

This rustic environment was not something he had seen in Salem, Massachusetts. He was used to seeing the hustle and bustle of the great ships arriving and departing the great seaport in the glory days when Salem was the largest seaport per person in the newly formed United States. He also saw grandiose brick buildings where the great merchants lived stretching down the road that ran along the harbor's coast.

His father was a sea captain who was part of the great shipping industry so it seemed that would be their life and he would live in an impressive brick home. But fate chose a different destiny for the young lad. Nathaniel's dad died from yellow fever on a voyage in the Caribbean when Nathaniel was four years old. He never really knew his father so his uncles, Richard and Robert, served as surrogate fathers.

After his father's death, he had lived with his Manning relatives in Salem on Herbert Street. It was close enough to the seaport that he could hear the chaos and clamor of the longshoremen and laborers on the docks.

When Salem was still recovering from the War of 1812, Nathaniel and his family moved to Raymond, Maine to live with the Manning family. Eventually, his uncles had a home built for Nathaniel, his mother and two sisters.

The vast woods around the home are a new world for Nathaniel. He was fascinated by it and wants to learn everything he can. He continues to go deeper into the woods, noticing a scattered clearing up ahead. He walks toward it but it seems so far away. He finally makes it there and he is surprised by what he sees.

"The ocean?" he questions in his mind.

The 12-year-old Nathaniel is shocked. They left the seaport and now they are near the ocean again. As he surveys the panorama, he realizes he sees mountains surrounding the water on one side and land all around the water. And there is an island in the middle of it.

"It's a gigantic lake; not the ocean!" he thinks.

Nathaniel has stumbled upon Sebago Lake and Frye Island. It is a name given to the lake by an indigenous tribe and it means "great stretch of water." The island is named for Capt. Joseph Frye who escaped a tribe of native Americans by jumping off a high ledge into the lake and swimming to the island.

Once again, Nathaniel is humbled by the awesome nature around him and practically overwhelmed. He sits down and just admires the vista. Thoughts pour through his mind as he imagines what could be on the other side of the lake and the island.

"Sights from a clearing," he muses.

Nathaniel catches something out of the corner of his right eye and turns his head to the right end of the lake. He doesn't see anything and is not sure what made him suddenly whip his head in that direction.

He scans the area and he starts to think it is a large animal. He saw a bearskin once back in Salem and remembers being terrified as he imagined the animal for real. He believes there is a bear in the woods. His heart begins to pound as he peers into the woods, looking for a pair of eyes gazing back at him as the light shades of sunset blanket the area.

He realizes that sunset is upon the day. The woods have become a little dark. He has lost track of the time and fears his mother will be furious. He has spent way too much time here and is now concerned if he can find the way back.

He tries to go back the way he came but it all looks the same. He notices a few landmarks like a rock that he sat on, a big hole and a fallen tree. It feels right to him and presses on. Finally in the distance, he hears his uncle shouting his name and heads toward the sound of the voice. He's home, but will get an earful for sure.

The next day Nathaniel returns to the woods but this time he has a knife and some string. His uncle gave him a lecture the night before on going into the woods alone and the dangers it presents. And he explained to him that there are bears in the woods. He is instructed on how to mark his path so he knows how to get back.

Nathaniel gets very adept at finding his way through the woods and likes to go to the clearing he found the very first day he that he ventured in. He enjoys the quiet of the woods and does some of his most formulative thinking there until he is torn away from these delightful days.

His mother and uncles inform him that he is being sent back to Salem to go to school. Nathaniel is acrimonious about this recrudescence and wages a series of protests. He counts down the days and tries to absorb as much of Maine as he can before he leaves at the end of summer to return to the city where he was born. Back he goes to the hustle and bustle that reminds him of his young childhood and the loss of his father.

The experience is nothing like the joy he feels when he is in Maine. Nathaniel is a loner and loathes Salem. A great portion of his disdain for the city where he was born is that his great, great grandfather was referred to as the "hanging" judge during the 1692 Salem Witchcraft Trials that sent 20 people to their death. He is ashamed of his family's past.

He writes letters home about the asperities of Salem and his discontent about being away from his family and nature. He can't adjust to the myriad of people around him. He wants the comfort of a quiet life like he had.

His pertinacious attitude finally persuades his mother and uncle to let him return to his true home, surrounded by nature, the lake and his family. He enjoys writing and pens a handwritten newspaper called The Spectator that is for his family and friends. His writings include essays, poems and news as well as his adolescent humor. He only writes seven issues but he is in his element; he is home and happy.

The happiness doesn't last long as his uncle demands that Nathaniel receive an education. The decision once again is met with protests. The anxiety he feels about going off to Bowdoin College is distressing, but he accepts this new chapter in his life. Nevertheless, this shy, reclusive young man makes friends, including a future US President at a train stop in Portland. Nathaniel and Franklin Pierce fast became friends and were together when Nathaniel passed away at the age of 64.

Everything seems to go well for Nathaniel until he graduates college. Change never sits well with him. He withdraws from the world, becoming reclusive again. He returns to Salem and stays in his room of his mother's home on Dearborn Street in North Salem. It's away from the harbor but near the banks of the North River. The activity on the river is less busy but still noisy. He is not talking to friends and family. He takes his meals in his room. But he is writing!

In 1828, he turns out his first novel called Fanshawe. It is a love triangle and it explains his withdrawal from the world. He appears to be writing about himself and some incident he had. The story is about a man named Fanshawe, who is weak and frail, who saves a woman from being murdered but declines to marry her due to his ill health and reclusive nature. The book gets good reviews but doesn't sell well. Hawthorne is despondent over the poor showing.

Nathaniel has no great direction for the next several years bouncing around to different jobs. He works as a magazine editor in Boston and then the Boston Customs House as a weigher and a gauger. But he decides he's going to marry Sophia Peabody of Salem, whom he has courted on and off for five years. He joins a commune to save money and they are married in July 1842.

Sophia is a transcendentalist. She is much less reclusive than Nathaniel; she writes and paints and has become a social butterfly. But she suffered from terrible migraines when she was younger and still has the occasional throbbing pain in her head. Upon being introduced to Nathaniel, it was as if her migraines went away.

Having suffered romantic loss while at college, Nathaniel immediately took a liking to Sophia. They were a good fit for each other. She brings him out of his shell a little bit and develops his delicate tenderness to understand the heart of a woman. He is manly enough to satisfy her and his brilliant, hypnotic blue eyes worked for her as well as many others

The newlyweds wanted a change in venue so they settled in The Old Manse in Concord. Massachusetts. The rent was a mere $100 a year. It was a lovely two-story home that used to be the parsonage 70 years earlier. The river flowed behind the home and there was a marsh next to it. Nathaniel was surrounded by nature and Sophia was near her transcendentalist friends. It was the perfect setting for the couple.

Nathaniel enjoyed taking strolls around and near the home. Sometimes with Sophia and sometimes without her. One day, he was out admiring the garden that Henry David Thoreau had planted for them as a wedding gift. There were various vegetables strewn amongst flowers that projected a pleasant aroma into the air that he found intoxicating.

Suddenly, he spied a tall man walking toward him. He watched as the man came closer, noticing his very long sideburns that just stopped short of being mutton chops. He thought of running away as he usually does in social situations, but it would have been incredibly awkward. Although, he was not opposed to manifesting such awkwardness.

Nathaniel once ran out the back door of the parsonage and into the woods when someone came to the front door. Another time, he was trapped upstairs when someone came to visit so he put a hat on his head and lowered the brim over his eyes, walking down the stairs, past the visitor and out the front door, leaving Sophia to apologize for his unusual behavior.

But Nathaniel was frozen this time. He was unable to escape and stared as the man finally stopped within a few feet of him.

"I am your neighbor Ralph Waldo Emerson," he began.

The shy Nathaniel extends his hand to greet his neighbor and introduces himself. In time, he was glad he had not run away for the two have much in common – the love of the woods and nature. It's another good fit for him brought on by Sophia's positive influence.

Waldo, a transcendentalist, already knew Sophia, so this led to them becoming close friends. He tells them about the history of the Old Manse and invited them into his social circle. Soon after, they are part of the Concord social scene. Nathaniel, however, is mostly quiet around big groups only opening up to certain people.

This little Concord social circle enjoys each other's company for over three years. They continuously meet at someone's home. Or they gather in the woods for a picnic amongst the beauty of nature. It is a wonderful time for honeymooners Nathaniel and Sophia.

But a chance encounter in the summer of 1845 changes Hawthorne on an innocent Spring stroll with Waldo. They meander through woods and down old roads until they happen upon the Hosmer Cottage, a school for children with a different approach than traditional schools. Nathaniel's shyness kicks in and he slowly veers away from the two men Waldo is about to greet.

"You have purposely walked me here Waldo," claims Nathaniel. "You know it is hard for me to meet new people."

"I did bring you here by design and I apologize for misleading you, but these are people I think you should meet," says Waldo.

Nathaniel grimaces but reluctantly follows his good friend. The introductions are awkward and Nathaniel makes as much small talk as he can muster before he feels he has spent enough time in the company of these new gentlemen. He gravitates toward the field as he hears the voices of young children saying words that are beyond their years.

He ventures closer and comes upon a group of children who are doing a play. He marvels at their playfulness, watching with admiration. And then he spies a young girl who is directing the play. He is drawn to her. There is something about her and he doesn't understand what he is feeling. He is enamored with her. She has skill and talent.

As he watches the children perform, he starts to get dizzy and then everything goes white in front of his eyes and he sees Sebago Lake. He is in the clearing where he spent much of his time. He is sitting there looking over the water when he sees something in the lake. He is not sure what it is but it frightens him. He continues to watch. He cannot turn away. Just as he is about to see what is in the water. He hears Waldo's voice.

"Nathaniel!" says Waldo. "Is something the matter?"

Nathaniel sees Waldo in front of him as well as another man that he soon learns is Bronson Alcott.

"I am fine," says a shaken Nathaniel. "But I probably should go home."

"You don't seem well," says Waldo. "Perhaps it is the heat of the day."

"Yes," Nathaniel says hesitantly. "The heat of the day."

He nods and bids farewell, but stops.

"Who is the young girl who is running this performance?"

"There?" points Alcott. "Oh, that's my daughter Louisa May."

Nathaniel doesn't explain why he asks the name of the young girl. He feels some sort of kinship that he doesn't think the father would appreciate. There is just something about her.

Not wanting to elaborate, Nathaniel bids farewell and makes his way back to the Old Manse. He enters abruptly and plops himself in a parlor chair bellowing Sophia for something cold to drink. Nathaniel is sweaty and full of anxiety. He is not sure what happened at the Hosmer Cottage.

Sophia brings him a glass of water and sets it down next to him.

"Nathaniel darling. What is wrong? You don't look well," she says.

He looks at her not knowing what to say and mutters some sort of assurance that he is fine.

"We'll that's good because we have company coming over soon," says Sophia. "Please go to the attic and fetch another platter."

Nathaniel is not in the mood for company especially now. He voices an argument that Sophia disregards. He begrudgingly goes to the attic to get a platter for his betrothed. He putters about up there looking in old trunks and boxes until he finds the platter she wants. But something catches his eye nearby. It has feathers and is soft. He pulls it out from the box and it is a stuffed owl.

The owl is various shades of brown with specks of white. Its tail is very long and dips below the six-inch pedestal on which its talons are perched. Its head is a darker brown. Its eyes are big and dark as the night. Nathaniel starts to feel the same way as he did at the Hosmer Cottage.

Suddenly, everything goes white and he is at the clearing at Sebago Lake. Again, he sees something in the lake. The water is bubbling. He starts to gasp. Nathaniel is paralyzed with fear as he tries to make sense of this daydream.

Sophia's voice snaps Nathaniel out of the trance he was in. He is not sure what this all means. He looks down and sees the stuffed owl in his hand. He lifts it up and stares into its deep black eyes. He cannot tear his stare away.

Sophia's voice is louder now, but he ignores her yells for the platter.

The box the owl was in is marked Harvard. There are more objects in the box. Waldo had told him many objects from the museum at Harvard College were moved to Concord when the British occupied Cambridge during the Revolutionary War. The owl must have come from Harvard.

"Found it," he yells down to Sophia, holding the platter and the owl. "Coming down darling."

Nathaniel trudges down the stairs with the platter in front of him while furtively hiding the owl behind him. He gets the taxidermic creature to the parlor where he proudly displays it on a table. He loves it as a conversation piece. It also reminds him of his days living on Pinckney Street on Beacon Hill in Boston when he wrote in a chamber he referred to as the Owl's Nest. Now he has a taxidermic owl to inspire him.

Nathaniel sits in the parlor staring at his curious find, trying to make sense of his childhood memories from the clearing. He is pensive and brooding at the same time. Sophia walks into the room, places the platter down on a table with a few snacks and spies the owl.

"What is that thing?" she demands in very ornery tone that Nathaniel has never heard before.

"It's an owl, my dear. A stuffed owl from Harvard," replies Nathaniel. "It reminds me of the days I wrote you love letters from the Owl's Nest on Beacon Hill."

Nathaniel's feeble attempt to tame his wife's outrage by recalling the love letters does not work to his satisfaction.

"It's disgusting and dusty," she says. "Get rid of it!"

"No!" says Nathaniel. "It's oddly charming. It's a great conversation piece for gatherings just like the one we are having. Our guests will relish the creature."

"It's ugly! I shall not have it in my home," says Sophia.

"I have already named it Longfellow after my college friend," says Nathaniel. "He will develop a keen fondness for it upon arrival."

Sophia storms out of the room and helps prep for her guests, who include Waldo, his wife Lidian, Thoreau, Margaret Fuller and, of course, Longfellow, who was amused by Nathaniel naming the owl after him.

The discussion amongst the guests is pretty much the same – the transcendentalist movement. Hawthorne concurs with some of the facets of the movement but raises concerns about some of the premises. They heavily believed in the philosophical, spiritual, and literary movement that emphasized the inherent goodness of people and nature, though Hawthorne expressed the opposite in some of his writings.

But the group thought that through the use of self-reliance and individualism, they could reunite with God. The discussion occasionally involved the plurality of worlds that theorized on life on other planets drawing Nathaniel into a sagacious inquiry on the matter.

Once all the guests had taken their leave, Nathaniel returned to the parlor and nestled into his favorite chair. He is on the precipice of an idea and tries to pull it into focus but it does not reveal itself as easily as he would hope. He is in a deep thought searching his memory, but it won't come into view. Sophia calls to him and jars him out of his self-imposed meditation.

Sophia and Nathaniel spend the evening together talking about the afternoon's event and occasionally reading some notes that Waldo had brought over. Every now and then Nathaniel wants to talk to Sophia about what is on his mind but he doesn't know how to broach the subject. He also fears his wife would think him mad. At one point, he notices the stuffed owl is not on the table where he put it. He looks at Sophia and chuckles to himself. He believes that she jettisoned it to the trash or threw it back into the attic.

The next day Nathaniel awakes and has an epiphany. He must talk to Louisa and broach the subject to her. The child will not think him mad. But how to talk to her is the issue. He feels it would be awkward to just walk up and talk to her about such a strange subject.

Weeks go by and Nathaniel's thoughts fluctuate about many things that have nothing to do with the conversation he wishes to have with the young girl. He is sitting in his study on the second floor of the Old Manse when Sophia calls to him. A courier has delivered a message.

"Nathaniel," Sophia says with curiosity. "We have a letter from someone I don't know. Do you know anything about this?"

Nathaniel trudges down the stairs while grasping the handrail. He is a bit miffed about having to break his concentration and stop his work. Sophia hands him the note that has been delivered.

"Your presence is graciously requested this Saturday at noon at the Hosmer Cottage for the opening of the play: "The Forest Animals."
– Louisa May Alcott

Nathaniel's disdain for having to abandon his work changes in a heartbeat. He chuckles at the message for fate has provided the answer for which he seeks. The young Louisa has reached out to him.

"We definitely should attend," he says to Sophia. "This is Bronson's daughter. I've seen some of her previous play. She is quite astute and a delightful child."

Of course, Nathaniel had a more secret reason for wanting to attend that he does not share with Sophia. He desires to talk to the young girl to see if she can provide any insights to his thoughts.

The week has passed and the play has arrived. Nathaniel is eager to go and believes Sophia does not suspect any ulterior motive, but she does realize he is looking forward to being in a group of people which is out of place for her shy husband.

Nathaniel and Sophia are the first to arrive. After a short greeting with Bronson and his wife Abigail, he plops himself down in the middle of the front row, patting the chair next to him for Sophia to come sit.

The small collection of 12 seats fills up and some people have to stand. They are all friends, family and acquaintances of the Alcott family. The play goes off and the crowd in attendance is thoroughly pleased with the children who perform. It lasts almost 20 minutes but it is a great achievement for this young troupe of thespians.

Nathaniel beams every time Louisa is on stage and evens lights up when the other children perform. Sophia notices that her husband is more open and emotional than he has ever been. When the play ends and the children take their bows, Nathaniel stands up and applauds, slowly followed by Sophia and the rest of the audience.

The children and the adults mingle to extend congratulations and discuss the play. Nathaniel and Sophia express their appreciation to the Alcott family and talk with Waldo and Thoreau. All the while,

Nathaniel bides his time to get Louisa alone to talk to her. He keeps an eye on her waiting for his chance.

When Louisa goes behind the makeshift stage, Nathaniel makes an excuse to walk away. It is the perfect opportunity. He strolls toward the cottage, looks around and detours to the back of the stage where he finds Louisa gathering up a few pieces of clothing.

"Hello Louisa," he says. "That was a wonderful play. I am most impressed."

Louisa turns around to see this man that she only had seen once before.

"Thank you, sir," she says.

"You may call me Nathaniel," he says. "I am Nathaniel Hawthorne. I live at the former parsonage."

"I do know who you are," she replies. "My father has spoken of you. He told me you are an author and I read your book Twice Told Tales."

"You have?"

"Yes. I really enjoyed Young Goodman Brown."

"Why thank you, Louisa. You are indeed a precocious child."

"I look forward to more of your writings."

"Oh, well that is indeed inspiring."

"Are you working on something now?"

"Yes. I am working on another collection of short stories and poems. I have no idea what I will name it but I will work the Old Manse in it."

"Well, I have to go to the house. It was nice to finally meet your acquaintance."

"May I just have another moment of your time? I wanted to ask you a question."

"Of course."

"What inspires you to write these plays? How do they come to you? I am very impressed that you can do these works at a young age."

"My father teaches me and my sisters Anna, Elizabeth and Abigail well. He has us study famous authors and we read works that adults read. That's how I read your book."

"Your father has a copy of my book?"

"Yes. He has copies of many books. We also read some of Mr. Emerson's work and Mr. Thoreau comes to teach his books too."

"Marvelous. Is there anything else that inspires you?"

"I am not sure what you mean. It just comes to me. I had a dream one time that I turned into another play."

"A dream? Very interesting."

"I really should go now. Father will be upset if I do not do my chores and studies before dinner."

"Very well child. You should pursue your studies and writing. I have the utmost confidence in your ability to pen greatness."

Just then Louisa drops a small pad of paper and it flays out to a drawing of trees.

"You draw as well?"

"Yes. I draw what I see in the woods."

Unbeknownst to Nathaniel, Sophia has come looking for him and spies him from afar as he flips through the sketch pad and happens upon one that strikes him. He shows it to her.

"This is most interesting," he says as he settles on one drawing.

"That is an owl I saw in the woods. I don't think it is a great drawing. I try my best. There's more in the back of the pad."

Nathaniel flips through the back of the sketch pad and sees owl after owl after owl.

"These are very good Louisa," he says. "Once again, I am dazzled by your prowess."

"Thank you, Mr. Hawthorne," she says. "You are most kind. I must be going now."

He hands her the sketch pad and she gathers her things and walks away. She waves to him and he musters a wave of his own as he watches her make her way to the cottage.

"What was that about?" asks Sophia, who has snuck up on her husband.

A startled Nathaniel is taken aback by his wife's presence and hesitates before answering.

"I was just telling Louisa how much I liked he play and she showed me her sketch pad," he says.

Sophia looks at him with a slight of suspicion for this is a side of Nathaniel she has not seen. She likes the newfound openness for it reminds her of when they first met. Her husband's conversation with Louisa May is the same from her perspective.

"I see," Sophia begins, accepting the explanation for the time being. "I enjoyed it. But the hour is late and we must return home."

The couple makes their final goodbyes and walks back to their home. Sophia prepares an easy meal of fruits, nuts and Banbury cake, a favorite of Nathaniel. As they finished partaking of supper, Sophia decides to pry into Nathaniel's thoughts once again.

"What exactly was going on between you and Louisa?" she asks.

Nathaniel is once again drawn to hesitation. He realizes that his wife knows more than he had believed. He struggles for an answer but she presses on.

"What are your reasons for your prolonged interrogation?" he snaps. "I was merely complimenting the young girl on her play."

"It seems to me you are enthralled with her," says Sophia. "There is something else afoot here."

Nathaniel considers telling Sophia about his visions but fears she will call the doctor and he will end up in an asylum. Yet, he owes her an answer to make her stop inquiring.

"I am enthralled with her as you put it," he confesses. "She is writing at this young age that is a great achievement. She is a rose in bloom."

"I've just never seen you act this way among children." she replies. "Perhaps we should have a child here in Concord."

"A child? Our first child," he says with a mock grin. "I suppose we could call the child Una."

"We'll see about that," she declares. "No child of mine will be called Una."

The conversation fades much to the delight of Nathaniel who does not want to reveal his secrets. Yet, he needs to figure it out as it engulfs his daily thoughts, causing him to lose focus and sleep.

Hawthorne tosses and turns that night. He awakes in the middle of the night and lays there staring out the window. He sees the woods lit by the light of the moon and admires the gentleness of the trees amongst the landscape. It takes a moment, but he realizes that it is the start of another moon cycle so there should be no moon visible in the night sky.

He rolls out of bed and goes to the window but there is no source of the light. He is befuddled yet compelled. Since he cannot sleep, he decides to get dressed and go to the woods. He has the same feeling of awe and wonder. He enjoys being close to nature; perhaps, a deeper love of nature instilled in him by Thoreau.

He becomes excited being in the woods. His pace quickens. The sound of leaves and twigs crunch under his feet. He picks up a stick he finds leaning against a tree to clear brush as he moves through the woods. He realizes it is the same as when he exploring the woods in Maine.

And just like that time at Sebago Lake, he sees a clearing. This time it is not empty. Standing in the middle of the clearing is Louisa May. It is the wee hours of the morning. He is shocked to see the young girl there. He runs up to her and kneels down.

"Louisa," he calls as she stands there with glazed over eyes. "Louisa!"

She breaks her stare and takes a minute to realize she is in the woods.

"Mr. Hawthorne. What are you doing here?" she says.

"That, my child, is the same question I have for you."

"How did I get here? Was I sleepwalking?"

"What do you recall?"

Louisa May tries to think but her mind is muddled. She stands in front of Nathaniel and shrugs her shoulders.

"You must remember something," he says.

"It's so foggy. I always have a good memory but I, I … wait. I do remember something."

"Yes, my child, what is it?'

"I was in a wheel barrel. No. It was a carriage. It was a small carriage."

"And was it pulled by horses?"

"No, it moved on its own. It was kind of like a train."

Nathaniel knows there is no train into the woods but turns his head both ways anyway to look for what she could possibly mean.

"No," she says. "Not a train on the ground. It flew. And there was a big owl in front of it directing it into the sky."

"Was this owl similar to the ones you drew on your sketch pad?'

Louisa May looks directly into Hawthorne's sparkling blue eyes. She has made the connection. Nathaniel dons a rare smile.

"What does it have to do with owls?"

"I am not exactly sure but I do not think it is anything to fear. Where did this train go in the sky,"

Louisa looks at Nathaniel and then gazes up toward the night sky with its hundreds of thousands of stars.

"Up there," she utters. "It brought me to a boat in the sky. It looked like the boat that goes across the Sudbury River at Fairhaven Bay. Father took us on it one time when we went to Marlborough for a lesson."

"A train and a boat," think Hawthorne. "It sounds similar to my short story The Celestial Railroad. Have you read that?"

"I'm afraid I have not read that book yet, sir."

"What else do you remember?"

"There were people there," she continues. "They were small like Elves. They were not much bigger than me. I think they were men but some could have been women."

"Little women and little men," Hawthorne inquisitively comments.

"They were teachers," she continues. "I was afraid at first, but a calm came over me when this one teacher spoke to me."

"And what did this teacher tell you?"

"Ideas. Lots and lots of ideas."

Nathaniel places his hands on her shoulders and stands up. He realizes now that he saw the same thing when he was at Sebago Lake in Maine. It was something that came out of the water and flew into the sky but not before it hovered in front of him. He remembers people that were more like creatures. And the thoughts that flooded his mind. He recalls one of them giving him the thoughts without speaking. Perhaps this is the teacher she references

He now understands why he was drawn to Louisa May. He solved their kinship. They are connected by way of a similar inexplicable experience. They have a bond through the teacher. Is it God? Has he reunited with God through the use of self-reliance and individualism? Has she?

"You need not be afraid Louisa. What has happened to you also happened to me when I was your age."

"Really? You flew on a train like me?"

"Perhaps," Nathaniel chuckles. "All I know is that I saw something similar when I was young. I think it is the same that you have seen and experienced. I had ideas after my experience but it took me time to act on them because I was unaware of what it meant. But you can act on yours. You are special Louisa."

"How will I know what to do with the ideas?"

"You will know when the time comes; it is within you," Nathaniel explains. "Every individual has a place to fill in the world, and is important in some respect, whether he chooses to be so or not."

Louisa May nods her head in affirmation and the exuberance of her youth is displayed upon her countenance.

Just then the two of them are bathed in a white light, prompting them to look up. They shield their eyes but cannot see anything that is causing the light. And just as quickly as the light shone, it disappears and there is nothing above them.

"What was that?" asks Louisa.

Nathaniel cups his hand on the side of Louisa May's face in a very fatherly way.

"That was the teachers saying goodbye. Now let's get you home."

∞∞∞∞∞∞

While the story of Nathaniel, Louisa May and extraterrestrials is fiction, there are many facets of truth to this story. Both Louisa May Alcott and Nathaniel Hawthorne lived fairly close to each other in Concord in the summer of 1842. Louisa May was 12 and Nathaniel had just turned 41.

Nathaniel did find a taxidermic owl in the attic of The Old Manse. He would display it for gatherings much to the chagrin of Sophia, who would hide it before gatherings. Meanwhile, Louisa May and her family lived at the Orchard House in Concord off and on from 1858 to 1877. She made several drawings of owls that are hung on the walls in her bedroom. Owls have been known to be a memory of alien abduction.

In addition, there is a picture of Rev. Samuel Sewall in her bedroom. He was her fourth great grandfather and a judge during the 1692 Salem Witchcraft Trials. Nathaniel's great, great grandfather was John Hathorne, who was also a judge during the trials. He was known as the hanging judge.

Louisa May started a newspaper at the age of 17 called the Pickwick. It was four pages long and included essays and poems. Nathaniel started a newspaper at the age of 16, called The Spectator. It too contained essays and poems.

Louisa May lived at The Wayside in Concord from 1845 to 1852. Her family called it The Hillside. When the Alcott family moved out, Nathaniel and his family moved in.

Both authors lived on Beacon Hill. Nathaniel lived at 54 Pinckney Street in 1839. Louisa May lived at 20 Pinckney Street in 1852 as well as a few other homes on the street. Her final years were spent living in a home at Louisburg Square, Boston.

The story is strewn with references to the books of Nathaniel and Louisa May, as well as quotes and family connections to entertain readers of both authors. Hopefully, these references shine through and provide the reader with the humor intended.

All of the coincidences and similarities cannot be ignored. Both authors definitely knew of each other and likely reconnected as adults as they travelled in similar social circles and lived in the same area. Whether they met in that summer of 1842 is conjecture, but very intriguing to think about.

VA BENE

(IT GOES WELL)

Francesca sits at a small circular table next to her kitchen window that overlooks the tiny backyard of her home in the North End of Boston. She slowly sips her espresso as she gazes out.

The memories of the octogenarian are mixed. She has spent her entire life here in this old Italian neighborhood living in an apartment on Tileston Street. Her view is mostly buildings packed together with a lack of green space, but she can see the Paul Revere mall where she would walk and sit with her husband and kids.

There are the shops where her mother took her when she was young. She took her own kids to those shops to maintain the tradition. She continues to go to the shops that remain from the old days. The church is visible a few blocks away as well as the community center where many gathered to pass the time.

Francesca took another sip of espresso.

And the festivals. She recalls in her mind all the festivals. Her first memory of the traditional feasts and parade was when she was six years old, watching people put money on the statue of St. Anthony. She would go to all the festivals because it made her feel good to forget all the bad times.

Francesca had a lot of struggles as did her husband Antonio. He was 24 when they married and she was 17. They were in love and had the whole world in front of them, but life together presented challenges.

Antonio had difficulty finding work from time to time as bigotry against Italians continued into the 1950s. Antonio's father was one of thousands of Italians detained during World War 2 for possibly being a spy for Italy. The family had to report weekly to the authorities and wasn't allowed to travel more than 10 miles from their home.

Antonio always remained bitter about that and felt people held it against him. Aldo was born a year after the couple married putting a strain on finances. However, they always seemed to manage.

But money got tight again when Isabella was born a year or so after that. Antonio found himself taking any job available to provide for his family. And again, they managed to get by.

Aldo was 18 when he was drafted for the Vietnam War. The family got word that he was killed a year later. Isabella was just 10 years old when she was killed crossing Commercial Street by a drunk driver.

Everything changed.

The pain that they felt was devastating. Francesca internalized all of her grief and Antonio lashed out more and more. He started to drink more. While he never abused his wife physically, he lashed out verbally, mismanaged money and was constantly angry.

Francesca kept mostly to herself and cried. She was always pensive thinking about the life she could have had. Since she vowed to marry Antonio "for better or worse," she continued to go about her duties as a wife. She was the good Catholic, taking care of Antonio despite all of the issues. And it continued for decades.

And now, Antonio was in the hospital. He had been there for almost a month fighting pneumonia and a host of other issues. It didn't look good. For the first time in her life, Francesca faced being completely alone.

She took her last sip of espresso.

Francesca breathed out a heavy sigh. She put her hands on the table and pushed herself up from the chair. She listed to her right as she slowly walked over to the sink to wash the cup. It was from a set that her mother had bought from Italy before she was born. She cherished that cup, carefully placing it in the rack to dry.

There was a knock at the door. Francesca wondered who could be at the apartment this early in the day. She was not expecting anyone. She made her way to the door. First, she unlocked the door knob, followed by turning the deadbolt open. She opened the door leaving the door chain lock on. Nobody was there.

Now she was curious and unclasped the chain. She opened the door wide so she could peer down the hallways. She looked in both directions. Nobody was there.

She stepped back into the apartment, closed the door and only reattached the door chain on since it was time to go. It must have been the radiator, she thought.

She put on her coat, grabbing her hat and purse. It was time to go visit Antonio in the hospital. Francesca never learned to drive. She wanted to but Antonio said having a car was always a luxury they couldn't afford. Public transportation was the only way for her to get anywhere outside of the neighborhood unless a neighbor drove. But she told herself she didn't mind.

Francesca had to walk to the subway stop, switch to another line and then take a bus. She couldn't get a seat on the subway and had to stand. She noticed how none of the men got up to give the old lady their seat. It took an hour for her to get to the hospital.

She walked into the lobby and was greeted by an employee who asked if she needed help. She waved them off because she knew the route by heart having done it twice a day for nearly a month. It was her routine to come and sit with Antonio in his room on the fourth floor for hours at a time. Sometimes he was awake and would talk to her but mostly he was unconscious. She would sit by his side as a good wife was supposed to do.

She arrived on the fourth floor and started to go to Antonio's room but was stopped by the nurse at the desk, who explained the doctor need to talk to her. She went into the tiny waiting room with five chairs and they were all taken. A young man saw her walk into the room and immediately gave up his chair.

"Grazie," she said to him as she sat. He just nodded and walked away.

The doctor came out from a room with a solemn expression. Francesca was fairly certain what that meant. And then the doctor confirmed what she thought. Antonio passed away a little over an hour ago. It seems to have happened when she was having her morning espresso.

Francesca was now alone.

No parents.

No siblings.

No children.

No husband.

She sat stoic. The doctor spoke but she was half listening. They gave her paperwork to sign so she scribbled her name. The doctor and nurse offered regrets and asked Francesca if she needed help getting home or with the funeral arrangements.

"Va bene," she told them. It means "I'm okay" in Italian.

Francesca used the bus and subway to return home. She first went to the church to tell her priest Antonio had passed. The church helped her with a funeral home and arrangements.

For the next few days before the funeral, Francesca had her morning espresso and sat by the window in her kitchen using her mother's cup. She did this for hours day after day until it was time for services.

The day of the funeral arrived and Francesca dressed completely in black like a good Catholic woman. It was common in Italy and many other cultures to dress in black while mourning a loss.

Sometimes your priest would tell you the mourning period was over. But some women would just continue to wear black and mourn for the rest of their lives. Francesca was in her 80s so she figured the rest of her life would not be that long so she planned to wear black until the end.

The funeral was sparsely attended by a couple of friends and a few community members that came to every funeral. The pallbearers were all from the church. Some were fine young men that she imagined how Aldo would be like. There was a small gathering at the community center organized by the church.

Francesca received condolences from many people; some that she didn't even know. A bunch of women from the church made food. She thanked everyone but just wanted to return home. After the gathering, her friends Carlo and Emilia walked her back to her home and carried up leftover food to the apartment on the third floor.

They sat at the table next to the kitchen window in silence. Carlo and Emilia offered words of kindness from time to time, but mostly they sat in solitude.

Finally, Emilia said that Antonio was a good man and it caused a notable change in Francesca's expression. It was like the rumbling you heard just before a volcano erupts. The widow looked at Emilia and just went on a rant.

All the internalized grief, pain and suffering for decades came out of Francesca in full force. She spoke in English and Italian.

"A good man? A good man? He was a good man for a few years!" she started in a very angry tone. "But then our Aldo and Isabella died."

"Era arrabbiato tutto il tempo," she said in Italian. "Non potevo dire nulla quando era arrabbiato."

He was always angry. I couldn't say anything when he was angry

"He was, come dici, down in the dumps," she cried. "I was too! Ho perso anche mio figlio e mia figlia."

He was, how you say? down in the dumps. I was too! I also lost my son and daughter

"He never talked to me about my feelings. It was always about HIM!" she yelled emphatically, gesturing with her left hand and then her right. "I had to make HIM feel better. I had to feed HIM! Dress HIM! And do what he always wanted!"

"Non mi lasciava fare nulla. Non siamo andati da nessuna parte. Restavamo sempre nell'appartamento."

He wouldn't let me do anything. We didn't go anywhere. We always stayed in the apartment

"Our 50th anniversary was wonderful," she happily recalled as her emotions dramatically changed. She leaned in toward Carlo and Emilia.

"We went to Ilario's Ristorante and had a nice dinner. The staff sang to us. It was the first time he had been happy in years. It was the first time WE were happy in years."

"Ma solo una volta! Il giorno dopo, he was back to being angry," she cried.

But only once! The next day he was back to being angry.

"Dovevo stare con lui a causa for better or worse," she lamented, raising the index finger of her right hand in the air. "Well, it was a lot more worse than it was better."

I had to stay with him because for better or worse. Well, it was a lot more worse than it was better.

She went on for close to an hour, never catching a breath while Carlo and Emilia sat there shocked. They had never seen Francesca like this ever. She was always quiet, never saying much about anything and being the good wife. They didn't know how to respond.

Francesca ranted, cried and sometimes smiled. But every change in emotion was saying the same thing. She missed Antonio, her kids and the opportunity she had for a happy life. She finally got decades worth of built-up frustration out of her system.

Francesca took a sip of espresso from her mother's cup. Silence hovered over the three of them like a heavy blanket. Carlo and Emilia sat there, looked at each other with a roll of their eyes and a slight shrug of their shoulders. They were unable to find any words of comfort for their friend.

During that exact moment of the tranquility, they all heard a voice come from the direction of the closet.

"Hai finito?"

It was Italian for "Are you finished?" They all heard it and it was unmistakably the voice of Antonio.

Francesca stood up and screamed, dropping her mother's cup to the floor where it smashed into pieces. She ran out of the apartment still dressed in all black and raced down to the church a few blocks away to pray to God and Antonio for forgiveness.

After a few hours at the church praying and talking to her priest, Francesca was calm. The priest forgave her and said that God and Antonio forgave her. She actually smiled for the first time in quite a while.

She left the church to come back home. She waited at the

crosswalk for it to change. She stood there waiting and thinking about the past and how many times she and Antonio had walked through the neighborhood. She recalled bringing a young Aldo and Isabella to the shops.

"Andiamo adesso," she heard in her ear. In Italian, that means "We go now." Francesca was somewhat in a trance and donned a rare smile on her face. She stepped into the crosswalk on Hanover Street into the path of a truck trying to make the light. She died instantly.

The church made funeral arrangements for her and the community helped. Carlo and Emilia were asked to go through Francesca's belongings. They spent a few hours in her apartment packing her things for the church to distribute to several charities.

Emilia lamented the loss of her friend to her husband Carlo, and they engaged in a quiet embrace. In that exact moment of silence, they both heard a voice come from the table next to the kitchen window.

"Va bene."

THE FINAL WORD

Marcus is sitting at a table outside a coffee shop on a beautiful Sunday morning in June. His head is buried in his phone. He's got an iced caramel latte sitting on the table. He slowly reaches out for it with his left hand, brings the straw to his mouth and draws the magic elixir into his mouth, all without taking his eyes off his phone. He places the coffee back on the table.

"Damn," he says under his breath as he shakes his head.

Samantha rushes up to the table and puts her hands on the back of Marcus' chair.

"You still haven't gotten it yet," she laughs.

"I will. I will," he says as Samantha grazes his arm with her sunflower sundress, taking a seat opposite him.

"You want a hint?" she asks.

"No," he says tersely. "I can do it."

She smiles at him as he struggles.

"You're enjoying this, aren't you?" he asks.

Samantha rolls her eyes and wears a smirk.

"No. I wouldn't say I am enjoying it," she replies. "I'd say it's more like relishing."

Marcus gives her the ha-ha look and shakes his head while putting the phone down on the table.

"I'll finish that later," he says. "What's up with you?"

Samantha goes into detail about the latest flack with her sister, mother and work. She is talking and Marcus isn't listening. Instead, he is smiling and looking at her. They are just friends and they decided that a few years ago, but Marcus still has a bit of a torch.

"So do you think I should call her out on that?" She asks.

Marcus is startled and struggles to answer.

"Well, ahhh, maybe wait a bit," he comments.

Samantha makes a face and nods. She has no idea that Marcus is still interested in her. She goes to get a coffee inside and Marcus picks up his phone again, trying to solve the puzzle before she returns.

After a few minutes, she returns and Marcus abruptly puts his phone on the table.

"Still no solve?" Samantha smiles.

Marcus waves his hand at his phone and says he'll figure it out later. The two of them start talking about a bunch of topics like friends do. Finally, they are done with their coffees so Marcus suggests they take a walk.

The pair stroll down the street and pass all sorts of different shops, occasionally looking in a window at merchandise. At one point, Samantha says she has to go in a second-hand store and check it out. She runs in and he follows. She gasps and grabs a hat that matches her sundress.

"What do you think?"

Marcus looks and the hat is perfect. It matches her sundress without a doubt. Samantha's blond hair drapes over her shoulders and is illuminated by the sun shining through the window behind her.

"It's you," he mutters from a trance.

Samantha buys the hat and is immediately transformed into an even happier person. They leave the store and walk down the sidewalk some more. They eventually cross the street and sit on a bench at the edge of the park.

"It's gorgeous out," she says.

Marcus nods. He looks around a bit and then asks if Samantha wants to walk the pass through the woods next to the park. Her demeanor suddenly changes.

"I don't like going in there," she explains. "Ever since that woman went missing. It gives me the creeps."

"She went missing in those woods," exclaims an astonished Marcus.

"They're not sure," she says. "But a few people said they last saw her in there. The police think something happened to her there."

Marcus agreed so they just sat on the bench for a few minutes more. They talked, watched videos on the phone and laughed. Finally, Samantha said she had to go. She was meeting her bestie for an art project they were working on for an upcoming festival.

They both stood up, embraced and said their goodbyes. Samantha walked away toward the downtown area and Marcus watched her fade into the distance, sun hat et al. He was definitely ensconced in the friend zone.

Marcus sat down and pulled out his phone. He went directly to the word puzzle. It took about 20 seconds before the epiphany struck. He entered his guess and voila, he solved it. He recalled his dad telling him that sometimes it's best to solve a problem by walking away and look at it hours later with a fresh eye.

He immediately texted Samantha the word. She responded with a smiley emoji, causing him to chuckle.

Marcus walked home and found himself alone. His roommates were still out. He looked in the refrigerator for a bite to eat but nothing. He looked around the kitchen but nothing struck his fancy. He opened the refrigerator door again in desperation that something would have magically appeared since the last time but still saw nothing.

Defeated and still hungry, he turned on his computer at the kitchen table and streamed a few videos. He was sad and bored.

He didn't like to be alone. He didn't like to be away from his friend Samantha.

He poked around on the computer some more and stumbled across a local news page with a story about the missing woman. Samantha was right about the woods. They didn't find her but they found her phone there. The police still weren't sure what happened and the woman was now missing for almost two weeks. There was a description of her and a picture as well as comments from family members asking the public for help in finding her.

Marcus felt sad for the family of the missing woman but that passed as his roommate James burst into the apartment.

"Hey Marcus. Still plenty of light out there. Want to go throw some hoops?"

Marcus smiled because he wasn't alone anymore. He nodded yes and the pair grabbed two bottled waters and headed out to the basketball court next to the park. Their other roommate, Terrell, joined them about 20 minutes later. After half an hour, more kids came to the court and they had themselves a full-fledged basketball game.

They played for over an hour until they started losing the sunlight. There were no lights around the court so they had to quit soon. The game ended as James sunk a three pointer. Marcus, who was six-feet tall, had been covering the smaller James, but didn't think his roommate could sink the shot so he gave him too much space. When the ball bounced off the rim and back down through the torn netting, Marcus hanged his head and his teammates were miffed. James came up behind Marcus and placed his hands on Marcus' shoulders.

"There's something you don't see every day," he whispers into his ear. "I'll admit it was a lucky shot."

Marcus turned and smiled at him. Some of the players continued to just shoot in the darkness, others went home, but Marcus, James and Terrell sat on the grass nearby, drinking the last of their waters.

"You hear about that woman that went missing?" Marcus asks, pointing in the distance. "It was right there in those woods."

James and Terrell shook their heads.

"Yeah, I have seen missing posters on telephone poles in the area," explains Terrell.

"Weird, right?" Marcus questions. "So close to where we live."

"Do they have any leads?" James asks.

"Not that I know," says Marcus. "I just read a story and they got nothing. Woman just disappeared. Found her phone in there. Samantha won't even walk in there because of it."

"Maybe she was murdered," says Terrell. "Or maybe she threw her phone there and ran away."

"She had a family with kids," explains Marcus.

"Doesn't matter," says Terrell, cutting off Marcus. "People leave their families all the time."

"It's starting to get late," says James. "We should get out of here and go back home."

The three picked up their things and the ball and headed home after a quick stop at the taco shack. Now the night was complete. It was close to 10 p.m. before they got back home.

Marcus started thinking about work on Monday morning. He hadn't had much success getting a job in the marketing field and had college loans to pay. He worked at a sheet metal factory trying to make ends meet. Meanwhile, James got a job in finance after school as did Terrell, but at a biological company working in a lab. Marcus felt he never had the same luck as his roommates whether it was a job, women or basketball.

"New information has become available about Marcia Simmons, the mother of two who went missing in the Buxton Woods two weeks ago," blares the TV as soon as James turned it on. "A second woman has now gone missing and police feel the two incidents may be connected."

Marcus slowly makes his way toward the TV as does Terrell. James plops down on the couch.

"Catherine Good was last seen on Thursday at the shopping mall on the east side of the city. Police are asking the public for help and the family has made an appeal."

"I really thought they were going to say the woods," remarks Terrell.

"Please," begins the family's appeal. "Please. If anyone has seen our daughter, please contact police. She was so kind. She was heading into her senior year in college. She loved animals and writing. She enjoyed playing board games with her family and games on her phone. Please help us find her."

The boys all looked at each other in disbelief. Two women missing in less than two weeks from the same little city. Sure, there were 40,000 people living here but that was a bit odd.

Marcus turned away from the other two and grabbed his phone, immediately texting Samantha to let her know. She replies instantly with "I heard. Tx."

"B. Careful" he texts back.

Marcus went to his room to go to bed. He had a little trouble sleeping because of the news story. He worried about Samantha, but he was also concerned for the two women. He wasn't sure if they ran away or if there was a serial killer out there. He hoped not.

Morning came and Marcus was up and out of the apartment before his roommates. He had to be in by 7 am because there was a big demand for product at the office and few workers. He didn't mind the overtime and extra money.

He got a break around eleven and used it to get a Jarritos mandarin soda and play games on his phone. He went straight to the daily puzzle, determined to solve it quicker than the previous day. This time he got it in four guesses thanks to a good starting guess. One of his better plays because he usually took five or six guesses.

He immediately texts Samantha.

"4 guesses 2 Day."

"2 guesses 4 me."

"U R so good at this."

"Tx"

Marcus returned to work and left around six. He walked near the woods and thought about going in to investigate. He stared at the woods for a solid minute, but decided that wouldn't be smart to do so alone so he went home. He was curious about what was going on in his city so he got on his computer and did some internet research on missing persons. He was surprised to learn that over 600,000 people go missing every year. Some don't want to be found, others are found alive and others are found dead. But the biggest portion, over 500,000, are never solved.

Marcus shook his head and continued to look at statistics. He checked his state and saw they were average. Then he checked his city and found it to be below average. Two missing women in two weeks was high. But he noticed nearby cities were average or better than average.

He tried to search recent missing people to see if there were more in the area that had gone missing but couldn't find any statistics. He wanted to see how many people in the area had gone missing in the first six months of the year and the years prior. He finally determined that those statistics weren't available.

He closed his laptop, got some dinner and hung out with his friends talking and watching a basketball game on TV. But he found his mind kept drifting to the missing person cases.

Wednesday morning came easily for Marcus. He was full of determination. He only had to work a half day so he decided he would try to find those statistics from the police. He figured what harm could come from it. He was a concerned citizen.

After his shift, he trekked over to the police station and asked for Detective Mascott, who was listed on the posters on the telephone poles. Marcus sat down and waited. He began to think maybe this wasn't a good idea.

Detective Mascott was a big man. He was about 6-2, 240 pounds and looked like an NFL linebacker. He approached Marcus.

"Marcus? I'm Detective Benjamin Mascott."

Marcus stood up slowly and shook the detectives outstretched hand hoping he wouldn't crush it. The detective ushered Marcus into a side room where someone was already sitting.

"This is Detective Anna Santos," says Mascott.

"Have a seat," says Santos. "You have some information for us?"

Marcus looked at the two detectives and realized his visit had been misconstrued and began second guessing himself.

"Ah, actually, no. I don't think so. I mean, I don't know anything, but I am ... curious," says Marcus.

The detectives look at each other trying to understand why Marcus is there.

"You see," he starts. "I was hoping you could tell me some statistics. I am very interested in these two cases because I am shocked that it is happening in my neighborhood."

"We can't tell you any information about an active case," says Santos.

"I know; I get that," says Marcus. "I just want to know how many people have gone missing. I was looking up info on the internet and this area seems higher than average for disappearances."

"If you know something, you need to tell us," Santos demanded. "Even if you think it is insignificant, it could help us solve these cases. What do you know that you are afraid to tell us?"

"I don't know anything. I'm just trying to understand and help," explains Marcus, getting up. "I should just go."

Detective Mascott had been standing against the wall and moved up against the table. His imposing frame towered over Marcus.

"Sit. Down," he says in a very calm voice.

Marcus sat right down. He was terrified of the detective.

"Where were you the night Marcia Simmons disappeared?" he asks.

Marcus realizes this was a mistake. Detective Mascott hunches over the table, closer to Marcus.

"I was at the basketball court sitting on a bench and I saw a light in the woods," says Marcus. "I'm not sure it was the same day she disappeared. It was a light. I don't know how to explain it."

The detectives checked in with each other once again.

"A light," asks Santos. "Like a lamp on a telephone pole or a flashlight."

"Just a change in the light. Like someone flipped a switch on and off," replies Marcus.

There is awkward silence as the detectives try to size up Marcus as a suspect, lookiloo or a fruitcake.

"Are there more than two people missing?" Asks Marcus.

"No," Detective Mascott says before he is cutoff by Santos.

"There is a third. A man. He was reported late last week. We have kept it out of the media," she says. "Do you know anything about that?"

Marcus shakes his head.

"Did he disappear in the woods?" Marcus asks.

"No," explains Santos. "He was last seen at the coffee shop near the park."

Marcus was stunned. It was the same coffee shop that Samantha and him go to. He begins to think he picked up on something or someone unconsciously.

"That's where I meet Samantha," exclaims Marcus.

"Is that your girl?" Santos asks.

"No. We're just friends."

The detectives gave Marcus their cards and told him to contact them with any information. Detective Mascott told him to not say anything about the third disappearance and Marcus agreed. He opened the door and Marcus left. He went home a different way figuring he was being watched by the police. As soon as he felt safe, he texted Samantha.

"How R U 2day?"

"OK. Headache."

"Sorry. Take aspirin."

"I did. No help"

"Lay down. Rest. Works 4 me"

"Yeah. When I get home."

"How did u do in game?"

"Two guesses."

"SMH. I took 4."

"You'll get there. Gotta Go."

Marcus made his way home and hung out with his roommates

again. This time they played Xbox and were killing zombies the entire evening.

Thursday morning came and Marcus was off to work early. He played the game on his lunch break and solved it in three guesses. He actually jumped up and cheered, drawing strange looks and chuckles from other co-workers in the lunch room.

He texted Samantha immediately.

"3 guesses"

There was no reply even after a minute. Marcus got a bad feeling, especially when five minutes came and there was no reply. But he had to get back to work, but he kept checking his phone for a response.

He texted her after work but still not response. He thought maybe she was just sleeping because she said she had a headache. Probably one of those migraines she gets from time to time.

Marcus texted her Friday morning and got no reply. He checked all day but no response at all. He didn't know what to think about being ghosted like this by Samantha. He felt something was wrong.

He went over to her apartment Saturday morning to check on her. If she were asleep, her roommates could let him know she was ok. As he turned the corner to get to her building, he saw a light. It wasn't like the woods. It was a flashing blue light of a police car. There were three police cars in front of the apartment.

Marcus freaked out and got a lot closer trying to figure out what was going on. Then he saw Detectives Mascott and Santos. Now he really freaked out. He wanted to leave, but he wanted to check on Samantha. Suddenly, he heard his name called. Detective Mascott had spotted him and called out to him.

Marcus put his hands in his pockets and slowly walked over to the detective, who summoned Santos who was interviewing someone who lived in the building.

"What are you doing here?" Mascott asks. "Do you know Samantha Rogers? Is that the same Samantha who is your friend?"

Marcus was freaking out. Strange thoughts ran through his head. He was going to become a suspect.

"Yeah," he mutters.

"Well, Samantha's missing for two days now so it is officially a missing person's case," explains Mascott. "And you are one of the last people to see her."

"We know you have a crush on her. And we also know she has a boyfriend and it is not you." says Santos. "You and her have an argument? And something went bad?"

"No … What? … No." Marcus yells. "I didn't do anything to her. She's a good friend. I care about her."

"You love her," says Santos.

Marcus pauses and looks at the detective for what seems to be an eternity.

"Yeah," he admits. "I love her."

The detectives look at each other evaluating Marcus, trying to figure if they make him for her disappearance. Marcus stood there with his hands in his pockets, looking at the ground.

"Detective!" yells one of the officers. "Here is her phone. We dusted it. Just her prints. Not even a partial of anyone else."

Marcus saw that the puzzle game was on the screen with a big "Congratulations, You have won!" On display. He realized that was the last thing she did on her phone.

"Don't. Go. Anywhere," scolds Detective Mascott.

Marcus shows his hands and complies because he is terrified of Mascott. He can't stop thinking that the last thing on her phone was the puzzle game two days ago.

"Marcus," yells Mascott. "Give us your phone."

Marcus hands it over and the detectives go through the text thread between Samantha and Marcus. They didn't see anything to implicate Marcus so they ruled him out as a suspect for now. He was free to go but he stood there, thinking what it all meant.

Then it struck him. He should talk to the family of the young woman who disappeared. Marcus left the scene and went home. He searched for the other two missing persons cases and found them and the addresses. He decided he would go to their homes and talk to the families.

It was a long walk across town but that gave Marcus plenty of time to figure out how to approach the situation. He kept going over it in his head. He didn't want to seem awkward and he didn't want people to think he was some sort of weirdo who may have something to do with the crime.

Marcus walked down her street and followed the numbers and finally came upon the home at the end of a cul-de-sac. It was a McMansion with a manicured yard with impeccable hedges encompassing it. The young woman came from money. He froze as he debated whether to go through with this or not.

Suddenly, the front door opened and a disheveled, threatening man appeared

"What the hell do you want?"

"I. Ahhh. I, ahhh, just wanted to…" sighs Marcus as he trails off on his words before stopping. He then walks away.

"Who the hell are you?"

At this point, the mother and son come to the door to see what is happening. Marcus turns around with his hands in his pockets.

"I'm no one," he says.

"Do you know my daughter Catherine?"

Marcus looks at the father, bows his head and walks away.

The father and the son came out of the house quickly and raced up to Marcus. They grabbed him on the arm and spun him around.

"Do you know something about my daughter?" the father pleads. He is less threatening and more hopeful, but his face is inches away from Marcus' face.

"No, I do not," he says.

"You're a bad liar," the son barks.

"What do you know about the disappearance of my Catherine?"

Marcus is shaken and the father releases his grip.

"I've been watching the news," says Marcus. "I saw you all on TV talking about her. And you said something that made me curious."

The missing woman's mother had followed her family outside to talk to Marcus.

"Curious about what?"

"You said she liked word games," he begins. "She played them all the time. She played that Wordsmith game on the phone. Did she play that day?"

The family looked at each other and then back at Marcus.

"It was on her phone in her car but she was nowhere to be found," explains the mother.

"She solved it. Right?"

There was an awkward silence as the family collectively gasped.

"Yes," replies the mother.

The son moves toward Marcus but being held back by the father.

"How did you know that freak? Nobody knew that but us and the police."

"My friend was just declared missing," says Marcus, who is cutoff by the father.

"There's another case?"

"There's four cases," explains Marcus.

The father's countenance turns again to being more threatening. "And how do you know all this?"

Marcus hesitates. Again, his attempt to help has possibly implicated him as a suspect. The family turned around and went back into their home, leaving Marcus in the center of the cul-de-sac.

"You stay right there," says the father as he points at Marcus. "I'm going to call the police."

He watched them go away and realized he stumbled upon the pattern. Two of missing person cases involved that damn app. They both solved it and disappeared. He suspected that the other two cases were probably the same.

Marcus walked the long trek home and thought about his next move. He wanted to tell the detectives, but he wanted to find Samantha. If they both solved the game and disappeared, he needed to solve it too to figure out what happened to them.

He got to his apartment and barely greeted his roommates, making a b-line to his room. He laid on his bed staring at the ceiling, trying to figure out how to solve the game. He thought about Samantha and how well she played it. His mind kept spinning. He finally drifted off to sleep.

Marcus sprung awake, but it wasn't morning. It was 3:33 am. His mind turned to the game and he realized it was a new game because it was tomorrow. The game starts anew at midnight.

He grabbed his phone and went to the app. He stared at the screen, wondering how anyone could solve it by randomly guessing the word on the first try. He looked up some stats and realized there are over 12,000 five letter words in the dictionary. It's impossible.

Does it have something to do with the day of the year? Perhaps some significance to a person or a holiday? He recalled how one day the answer was "ghost" on Halloween. He laid down and racked his brain. He had nothing. But that screen beckoned him.

He suddenly sat up with an idea. I'll cheat, he thought. People post the answers all the time.

Marcus did a search and came up with a website in seconds. He clicked it but it wasn't updated for the new game. It was early morning. He checked a few other sites and it was the same. No update. He would have to wait.

He tried to go back to sleep but it was no use. He tossed and turned, checking the cheat website every 20 minutes. Morning came and still no update. He had to go to work so he got dressed and bolted out the door, barely talking to his roommates.

He was almost to work when he checked the cheat website and it was updated. He had the word. He was excited and nervous at the same time.

Marcus sat down on a nearby wall and went to the app. He looked around as it loaded. He took a deep breath to calm himself. He slowly typed in each letter, careful not to make a mistake. He was like a Wheel of Fortune player enunciating every syllable clearly to win the game.

He hovered over the enter button with his finger. Then he took a deep breath and pushed the button, waiting to see what would happen.

The app displayed all sorts of graphics of balloons, people cheering and the word "congratulations." Marcus looked around and nothing seemed different. He then heard a different sound from the app.

He looked down and much to his chagrin, there was a message in the middle of the display.

"You cheated!"

Marcus watched in horror. He realized he looked up the cheat word on his phone and played the app on his phone. There must be an algorithm that lets the game know. The app is being monitored.

"You must earn it to be saved."

What the hell does that mean? thought Marcus.

"You have one day left to be saved before the solstice."

A wide-eyed Marcus was totally perplexed. He checked his phone calendar and realized the solstice was tomorrow morning before noon. He searched the internet and read about the solstice. It is the first official day of summer because the Earth's poles have their maximum tilt toward the sun. The solstice was celebrated in many cultures with festivals. It was key in early agriculture. And some cultures thought the end of the world would occur on the solstice.

"Good luck."

"Oh, hell no," Marcus says aloud. "End of the world? That's some bullshit."

After several minutes of contemplating what this all meant, he got off the wall and called in sick to work. There was no way he was going to spend his last day working. If this is his last day. He debated telling the detectives. His roommates. His family. Nobody is going to believe me, he thought. He'd be branded a lunatic.

Lunatic; that's funny, he thought. That's what they called people affected by the moon. This has to do with the sun. He'd be a Sunatic or is that Solartic?

He wasn't sure he believed any of this.

Marcus strolled around the city and found himself at the coffee shop that he would go to with Samantha. He ordered a Caramel Frappuccino with whipped cream.

"Would you like any toppings on that?"

Marcus thought about it.

"Yeah," he says. "I think today is the one day to splurge. Throw some chocolate bits on top of that. And I'll take a blueberry muffin."

The young woman filled his order and Marcus chuckled. My last day on earth and my idea of living it up is going all out at the coffee shop, he thought.

Marcus sat outside trying to make sense of everything. He had one chance. What could tomorrow's word be? The solstice. He went to the internet on his phone. Then a message popped up.

"You're not smart enough to figure this out."

He wasn't on the app but was getting push notifications.

"Sit back and enjoy your last Caramel Frappuccino."

Marcus spun his head to the left and then to the right, looking around the coffee shop trying to determine if someone was there watching him. He saw a student on a computer doing some work and two older women having a coffee. He looked at the security cameras in the shop. But then he realized he had paid for the coffee with his phone. Everything he did was being monitored by the app. Who is behind this app? He so wanted to respond, SMH.

He just sat there. He was numb thinking about Samantha, the end of the world and the final word. Then he wondered if he wanted to be saved. Where do you go? What's going to happen? Is this God or the government? Or is that one in the same? Do we go to heaven?

He searched "heaven" on his phone and read a bunch of information from cultures all over the world.

Suddenly, a push notification came up.

"Heaven, huh? What makes you think heaven wants you."

"You trash-talking me?" Marcus screams. "I don't need this from you. I'm going to beat you Mother******."

Marcus realized he was yelling into his phone and several people turned around staring in awkward wonder at Marcus, the sunatic. He raised his hand to settle people down and apologized. People probably thought he was having an argument with a friend, when he was really fighting with this app.

Then he spied Detectives Mascott and Santos across the street in their car watching him. His heart sunk. He realized the family of the missing girl called the police and that they have been likely trailing him for a while.

He decided to leave and walked through some backyards and alleys trying to throw off the detectives. He figured he couldn't go home because the detectives knew where he lived. He decided to go to the library to use the computer so the app can't track him. He had to figure this out. He didn't care about being saved from whatever was going to happen. He wanted to see Samantha again.

He entered the library through an employee entrance. He found a computer station in the corner of the library away from other people. He logged in as a guest and started searching solstice, reading page after page of information. His mind raced. Solstice is Latin for "sun still." Maybe still. What goes with sun? Sunset. Sunrise. Sunshine.

He opened up an anagrammer online and entered sun with two question marks. And a few more possibilities came up. Sunup. Sunny.

What goes with sun, he thought.

Light. Glare. Flare. Solar.

That's got to be it, he thought.

Just then he heard some people talking to the reference librarian. He peered over the study carrel and there were detectives Mascott and Santos. He ducked down before they looked in his direction.

"This isn't good," he thought.

Marcus needed to get out of the library. He decided to go back home since the detectives probably already went there. They wouldn't look there again for hours. He planned his escape and then he got a loud notification on the computer.

"You can run but you can't hide."

Marcus rolled his eyes and feared the notification was so loud that the detectives heard it. He carefully weaved his way around the carrels and bookcases to go out the door he had entered. He ducked around the corner and slipped into a backyard and hustled home.

He burst into the apartment and went to his computer, but stopped. He grabbed Terrell's computer because he thought the app probably had an algorithm to his computer. And he knew Terrell's password. He logged in and resumed his research.

"It's either solar, sunny or shine," he says aloud. "But I think it is solar."

He sat back and felt confident for a moment and then started second guessing himself. He paced around the room a bit and then grabbed a bottle of tequila and plopped down on the couch to do some day drinking. After two shots, he laid his head on the couch and closed his eyes.

"What are you doing home early?" James asks as he shuffles into the room.

Marcus awakens slowly and wipes his eyes. It's been a few hours.

"Are you okay?" asks James

Marcus looks at James and has no idea how to answer the question.

"Yeah, I'm okay," he mutters. "I just stayed home today."

Marcus contemplated telling James what he knew, but why should he make James feel miserable like he felt. Spare him the anguish, he thought, and it will just end quick.

Terrell came in 10 minutes later and tried to get his roommates to go down to the basketball court for a game. But James said no and Marcus certainly wasn't in the mood.

A push notification chimed rather loudly on Terrell's computer

"You figure it out yet champ?"

Terrell walked over and looked at the message.

"What's going on man?" Terrell asks. "You got a bottle of tequila on the table and you just got a weird message on my computer. Who said you could use my computer?"

Marcus looked at them. He thought of saying something but decided against it.

"I just need some air," he says as he gets up and walks to the door.

Before he goes out the door, he turns to his friends one last time.

"I just want to let you both know that I consider you my best friends," he began. "You're my brothers and I will always cherish our time together."

James and Terrell looked at each other as Marcus walked out the door. Marcus hustled down the stairs before they could come out and stop him. He wasn't sure what he was going to do and where he was going to go. He just wandered around the city.

After a few hours and the sun started to dip, he decided to go to the woods near the park. He figured the woman disappeared there and Samantha wouldn't go there so maybe that meant something. He would enter Solar in the app, while sitting in the woods.

He entered the woods, keeping alert in case of animals, other people or something worse. He found a little clearing and sat down on a fallen log. And then he heard some yelling. His friends were looking for him and calling his name. He checked his phone and realized it was nearly 11 p.m. One more hour and he could take a shot at the final word.

The sounds of his friends calling his name began to fade. The time passed slowly. Marcus looked at the time over and over again. He was experiencing a range of emotions he couldn't comprehend. He felt worn out. He slid down the log and laid his head against a tree that butted up against the log. He adjusted into as comfortable a position as he could and closed his eyes.

Marcus heard a twig snap and sprung awake. He didn't move, but looked in every direction. He felt like he dozed off for 20 minutes but was surprised to see it was almost 2 am. He could enter the word.

Marcus pulled his phone up to his chest and opened up Wordsmith. There it was. Ready and waiting for him. He hovered over it with his right forefinger for a moment and then pulled back.

This is insane, he thought. What am I doing?

He began to think of everything that brought him to this point and what it all meant. He began to think of Samantha.

Just do it, he thought. It must be the correct word.

He started again. He hovered over the screen with his finger and then began entering the letters.

S-O-L-A-R

He hovered over the enter button. His finger drew closer. He took a deep breath, closed his eyes and pressed the button.

He felt a bit of heat and sensed a change of light through his eyelids. It all felt right. He opened his eyes, saw the morning sun and Samantha standing in front of him. He was stunned.

"Samantha," he spoke aloud. "It's you. I'm so happy to see you."

He reached out and grabbed her arm.

"I missed you so much," he cries.

"Yeah, I missed you too Marcus," replies James.

"What the hell are you doing out here?" Terrell asks.

Marcus pulled back and looked around.

"Where did she go?"

"Who?"

"Samantha!"

Terrell and James looked at each other.

"Samantha's gone Marcus and it doesn't seem like she's coming back," explains James.

"But the game. We all have to get the word to save us from the end of the world," screams Marcus.

His roommates are baffled as Marcus babbles on about everything that has happened and that the game is picking people to survive the end of the world.

"Let's get you home buddy," says Terrell.

They each get on one side of Marcus and start escorting out of the woods. Marcus continues to tell his story but they just don't listen. He's getting inconsolable as he makes his case.

Suddenly, their cell phones each sound off with the national emergency ringtone.

Breaking News: A massive solar flare has erupted on the sun and it is headed toward the earth. Get inside. Prepare for disruption of all electronic devices.

"This is it!" Marcus screams. "This is what I was telling you about. It's happening."

Terrell and James don't want to believe it.

"I failed," says Marcus. "I typed S-O-L-A-R. I bet it is F-L-A-R-E."

They stare at him.

"Open up the game and play it!" Marcus yells.

"What about our families and friends?" They ask.

"I'll email them. You play the game," says Marcus.

James enters the word F-L-A-R-E and he gets the congratulations on his phone. There is a light emanating from what appears to be a portal in the middle of the woods. It is blurry and wavy. It almost looks like when you first pour milk into an ice coffee and it swirls around looking like a stormy, cloudy day. They can see through it to the park on the other side.

"Go into the door James," yells Marcus.

James looks back at Terrell, who is still downloading the app. He enters the word and another portal opens up. Terrell is reluctant but Marcus gets up and pushes him in. James and Marcus share one last look.

"Just go," says Marcus. "I'll be fine."

James nods and goes into the portal. Both of Marcus' friends have disappeared and the portals are gone. Marcus emailed his roommates' families and everyone in his contacts to play the game and enter the word F-L-A-R-E. He posted it on the internet in some community and gaming groups.

Marcus turns and, in the distance, he spies a black void. It seems to be swallowing up everything in its path. He realizes there is nowhere to run or hide. He stands there watching as this darkness erases everything from the horizon as it comes closer.

A push notification suddenly appears on his phone. It's fading and hard to read as the signal is waning.

"There may … be … hope for you … yet, Marcus."

Marcus looks at the message and just smiles.

The black void draws closer. Marcus watches as a family in the path gets swallowed up. They are gone. Marcus gasps.

Marcus grabs his phone and goes to his photos. He calls up a picture of him and Samantha at the beach. It is one of those photos you call a keeper because it is a solid memory of joy. He smiles as the black void is even closer. It will be on him in seconds and he will be erased.

Suddenly there is a light change. A portal opens up behind him about 10 feet. He turns to see it. He doesn't understand why but he runs toward it as fast as he can. The black void is getting closer and closer. Marcus is getting closer to the portal. It's going to be close. Marcus is giving it everything he has.

He gets close enough to the portal while the black void nips at his heels. He launches himself into the air and dives toward the portal. It's as if he is a baseball player diving toward first base trying to beat the throw from the shortstop.

And suddenly Marcus feels the weirdest sensation he has ever felt in his life.

Mail Call

Lauren is staring out her office window at the sun-soaked parking lot. She has a corner office on the third floor, but her only window looks out upon another building. If she cranes her neck just right, she can see the glistening water of the Charles River. She sometimes would stare at the window of the office across the way and could get a better view of the water. However, those folks grew tired of her staring and closed the blinds.

She sits there in her leather chair with no motivation to work. It's almost time for the weekend to start. Just 30 minutes and she can bolt out of there. The SEC reports for the bank will wait until Monday. They are not due yet anyway.

Her head rests against the upper section of the chair. She closes her eyes and waits a few seconds. Reluctantly, she digs her heels into the carpet and spins her chair slowly around until she faces her desk as if she was going to work. She opens her eyes and screams.

"I am so sorry Miss Costello," said Carl from the mailroom in a very flat, monotone voice. "I thought you heard me come in."

Lauren takes a deep breath. She wasn't expecting Carl to be there. She didn't hear him walk in. She never hears him walk in. He seems to do this often whether it is in her office, the lunch room or elsewhere.

"It's okay. I shouldn't have closed my eyes," she blurted out. "What do you want?"

Carl stood there with his arms motionlessly hanging straight down against his grey corduroys. She couldn't see his hands because they were below her desk. The mail cart he used was in the hallway. It seemed like an eternity for him to answer.

Lauren looked at him just waiting for him to finish. He spoke slowly and deliberately. He was very quiet and he tended to wear bland clothes. She called him Creepy Carl. She never said that to his face or to co-workers. She had mentioned him a lot to her boyfriend Jake and to her girlfriends, but she didn't want to risk anyone in the office letting it slip out because she never wanted him to find out. She wasn't concerned about his feelings. She was afraid of him. He was creepy.

He slowly raised his left hand. Lauren's eyes widened as his hand breached the top of the desk. It was a very thin clasp envelope.

"This came for you," he said. "It arrived after the first mail. It looked important. I figured you'd want it right away."

He handed it over to her and she cautiously grabbed it. He didn't let go of it so they both were holding the envelope at the same time. He smiled at her as if they were holding hands. She gave it a little tug and he let go.

"Huh," she sighed as she looked at it.

"Not important," Carl asked as he leaned over her desk enough to make her lean back in her chair.

"No. I mean, yes. It's important. But not too important," she said.

"I shouldn't have bothered you with it," Carl said, still leaning over her desk. "I feel so ... bad."

Lauren just wanted this exchange to be over and him gone.

"It's fine Carl," she said, averting her eyes. "I needed it. But I have to go now. I'll deal with it Monday."

She stood up and grabbed her purse. She fumbled through her purse and never looked up again, just hoping he would leave. He finally took the hint but it took forever.

"I'll be going then," he said as he turned to go. "I'll see you at next mail call."

Lauren did not look up until she heard the wheels of the cart roll away. Even then she only peeked to make sure he was gone before she raised her head completely. She knew he had a crush on her, but never in a million years.

Her heart belonged to Jake. She had only met him less than a year ago but he was dreamy. He was athletic having played baseball in the minors but never made it to the big leagues. That was okay with her because he was very fit and very muscular. She wished she could see him tonight, but he was doing a camping weekend with his buddies up in New Hampshire.

It was pre-arranged and she was fine with it but she had nothing to do tonight. All three of her close girlfriends were busy with other commitments. She would just go home on a Friday night. Maybe she would pick up some dinner and watch a movie. But nothing scary because she just had to deal with Creepy Carl.

She slung her pocketbook over her shoulder and walked to her door. She gave her office a final look as if she was forgetting something. She looked and the safe was locked, all the files were put away and nothing was on her desk. Bank policy was that nothing is left out on your desk because of the sensitivity of account information. She was responsible for foreign account transfers. She had a very important fiduciary responsibility to make sure the information was safeguarded or it could cost her job.

She swung the door closed and tried the handle. It was locked. Good. She walked away but only got three feet when she went back to the door and tried the handle again. She became very pensive before she tried it, whispered the word chrysanthemum and then tried it. Locked.

Lauren said the name of a different flower every time she locked her office door. It was her way of remembering it was locked. She would wake up in a panic some nights thinking she had forgotten and had envisioned her door wide open and client information at the ready for anyone to walk in and take. Then she would remember the word she uttered and would calm down.

It was anxiety but that's what made her good at her job. Chrysanthemum, she said to herself as she walked away.

She made her way down the hallway toward the elevator. She debated about taking the stairs since the elevator was always slow. She wanted to get out of there but she didn't feel like going down a few flights with her heels. The doors finally opened. The elevator was empty. She hurried in and pressed the button for the first floor, followed by the pressing of the door close button a dozen times.

Finally, she thought.

Her mind started thinking about evening plans. Maybe she would stop at the new Mexican restaurant that just opened up down the street from her condo and have a margarita.

The elevator door opened on the first floor. She looked up and saw a few co-workers walk past her. She stepped out into the hallway and made her way toward the security guard desk that was positioned in front of the employee exit.

"Not bringing home any work this weekend? Nice," the guard said.

She managed a smile and shifted into a better mood as she showed the guard her open purse.

"Have a good weekend," he said.

She waved her hand goodbye and as she did, out of the corner of her eye, she saw Creepy Carl at the end of the hallway with his mail cart looking directly at her. Her improving mood suddenly worsened.

Maybe two margaritas, she thought.

She turned and walked out the employee exit. She was a bit frazzled and forgot which way to go. After looking in both directions, she finally realized which way to go to get to the garage. It was only around the corner. Just a short walk to freedom.

Hmm, Watermelon margarita sounds nice.

She saw the elevator but took the stairs. She didn't care for the garage elevator, especially if she was alone because employees from other companies in the building used it too. Walking up the stairs in heels was easier than walking down but there were many cracks that heels could get stuck in. Her gray skater skirt swung back and forth as she carefully ascended the stairs. She got to the second floor quickly and then darted over to the section of the garage that faced the Charles River. At least her car had a view of the water even if she didn't from her office.

Lauren got halfway down the side of the garage when she started scanning for her car. The corner of the garage was just ahead and she didn't see her blue Fiat 500. She loved her car even if her friends didn't. They joked that Fiat stood for Fix It Again Tony. But she knew it really meant Fabricco Italiano Automobile Tourino (Italian made touring car).

She stopped and turned and it wasn't there. She was certain she parked it on the second floor. She was in early and there were plenty of spaces on the second floor. She was certain, but her car wasn't there.

Maybe I parked on the third floor, she thought. She looked over toward the stairs and it seemed so far, but every long journey begins with a first step. She chuckled to herself thinking she must have been still groggy when she got in so early.

Perhaps a coconut mango margarita, she thought.

She went up the stairs to the third floor and walked over to the river side of the garage. Again, her car was not there. She turned around looking in every direction and was dumbfounded. Maybe it was stolen. This was so unlike her. She saw a car coming down from the third floor. She turned toward the river again.

No way I parked on the fourth floor, she thought.

She made her way toward the stairs. She was thirty feet away when she heard the car from the fourth floor slowly coming up behind her. She moved to her left and she sensed the car moved to the left too.

What the hell? She thought. There's plenty of room. She turned and she couldn't believe her eyes.

"Carl?"

There he was. Creepy Carl in his creepy car – a beat up 2009 Ford Taurus. The window was down and Carl had that strange look on his face that she usually saw in the office.

"Everything ok?" he asked.

She was caught off guard and hesitated to answer. She never wanted to give him an opportunity for further conversation.

"I can't find my car," she blurted out, realizing her mistake. "I think it's on the next floor."

Carl smiled. Lauren was slightly vulnerable and he took his shot.

"Get in my car," he said. "I'll drive you up."

Lauren searched for a way to get out of this.

"I don't want to trouble you. It's only one more flight up," she said. "The stairs are right there."

She started walking and Creepy Carl paced her with the car. It looked like some odd race that the host country of the Olympics gets to add.

"No. It's okay. Thank You. It's okay," she managed. "I guess I have been working too hard."

"Are you sure?" Carl questioned, leering at her legs. "You've been walking up the dangerous garage stairs from the second floor in those heels. You must be tired."

Lauren turned and put on a big fake smile.

"You are so kind," she beamed. "But it is really no trouble. My own foolishness. But thank you so much Carl for the offer."

She sped off and got to the stairs as quick as she could. She felt light headed as she made her way to the fourth floor. She turned the corner and looked. There it was, facing the river on the fourth floor. The sun was beating down on it and that was something she didn't do because it made the leather seats too hot.

It was so strange, but she was happy she found her car. She aimed her remote and pressed the button. She grabbed the handle and it was locked. That meant she just locked it with the remote. It was unlocked all day. She was flummoxed at this point. It made no sense to her, but she didn't care. It was Friday. She was out of there. After all, margaritas awaited her.

Lauren backed out of the space a little too aggressively, shifted forward and started her descent down the four levels. She stopped at the gate, rolled down her window and pressed her pass against the magnetic pad to freedom. She headed to the highway to get to her suburban condo and the comfort of her familiar surroundings.

She reached cruising speed and switched on her iTunes and on came Bruno Mars. It took a few lyrics and then she sang along.

> "When I see your face
> There's not a thing that I would change
> 'Cause you're amazing
> Just the way you are
>
> And when you smile
> The whole world stops and stares for a while
> 'Cause girl, you're amazing
> Just the way you are."

Singing always made her feel better and this helped her shake off the entire incident with her car. She was now in party mode and could taste the margaritas. And then all of a sudden, it hit her like a ton of bricks.

Creepy Carl said she had been walking up the dangerous garage stairs from the second floor in those heels. How did he know? He came down from the fourth floor. How could he have known that?

She shut off the tunes to think. She would have taken the elevator if she was on the fourth floor. She walked up the stairs because she was on the second floor. Did he watch her as she left the building? How could he watch her and have time to go to the fourth floor and get his car?

She was puzzled, but kept racking her brain. What if he moved the car from the second floor to the fourth floor to make her walk up the stairs? But he couldn't have done that. She had her keys with her in her purse all day. It wasn't out of her sight. But the car was unlocked. She always locked it.

Lauren convinced herself that Creepy Carl had moved her car. She had kept speeding up in the fast lane as she was lost in thought and was well over the speed limit when fear gripped her. She took one brief look over her shoulder and then cut over three lanes to take the next exit. She envisioned Creepy Carl sitting in her driver's seat, moving her car. She ignored the blare of a few horns, took the exit and parked across a few spots at a strip mall.

She flung open the door and got out of the car. She figured she looked like quite a spectacle as she jumped around like a spider was on her. But it was no spider; just the thought of Creepy Carl sitting in the driver's seat of her Blue Fiat 500. That was something Tony couldn't fix, she thought.

After a few minutes, she calmed down and decided she wanted Jake. She grabbed her cell and called him. As soon as he answered, she started in.

"Jake! Jake! Creepy Carl moved my car from the second floor to the fourth floor and is stalking me and maybe made a copy of my keys and is waiting for me at my condo," she said.

Jake processed what she said. She started again and he interrupted her.

"Wait a sec!" he said. "What happened?"

She explained it all again in further detail. She was a little frantic but very systematic in how she explained it. Jake didn't put up any arguments like he had before. He had told her it was simply in her mind, but now he realized that she had a logical argument.

"I'm not going back to my condo," she said. "He must have a copy of my keys."

Jake did his best to assure Lauren that Creepy Carl was not stalking her, but it wasn't working.

"Ok. Go to my condo," he said. "I'll meet you there. I'll leave here in 10 minutes. I should be there in 90."

Lauren calculated that she would be alone in Jake's condo for approximately 40 minutes before he arrived and it wasn't good enough.

"I know," he said, "but I can't change physics. It'll be fine."

"I'm afraid this guy is really stalking me Jake," she cried.

He thought for a moment and then spoke.

"I left my gym bag in the trunk of your car. Inside you will find a pouch that is locked. The combination is the first six numbers of my cell. Open it. You'll find my gun."

"I've been driving around with your gun in my trunk," she scolded. "That is so irresponsible. I could get arrested."

"It was either that or leave it at my office," he defended. "It was safer in your car. But now, you have a gun and you can protect yourself."

Her anger melted away because he was right. She had a gun in her possession and he had taught her how to use it. She had taken the basic safety course and went to the shooting range with Jake several times. She could defend herself.

"I'll see you in 90 minutes Lauren," he said.

"Okay," she said. "Hurry. I love you."

"I love you too," he replied.

Lauren hung up the phone and grabbed the gym bag out of the

trunk. She reluctantly slid back into the driver's seat where Creepy Carl's ass had once been. But she had a gun and she'd put a cap in Creepy Carl's ass without hesitation.

She opened up the bag and saw the pouch. She worked the combination, undid the lock and pulled out a 9MM. She lifted her head and looked to make sure nobody was watching. She held the gun low below the windows anyway. She checked the clip and chamber and they were empty. There was a small pack of bullets in the pouch. She would wait to load the weapon until she prepared to enter his condo. She slid the gun back in the pouch and pushed it farther into the bag, revealing a pack of cigarettes.

He's still smoking, she thought. He lied to me. He said he stopped. I'll deal with that later, she thought.

Lauren hated cigarettes which was somewhat ironic because she smoked in college. She was younger then and everyone smoked. She gave it up a few years after college and became one of those former smokers who are adamant anti-smoking advocates. Smoking was a deal breaker for her, but Jake hid it from her for five months. Despite this, she fell into a relationship with him and he promised to quit for her.

She directed the car out of the parking lot and back onto the highway. Jake's condo was 50 minutes away. She had to drive up Route 128 during rush hour and it would be brutal. She would get to his condo a little before 8 p.m.

She pushed the pedal a little harder but didn't put on any music. She was in her own head now and was determined to reach her destination asap. She caught herself looking at the gym bag. It wasn't because of the gun; it was the cigarettes.

She was thinking of smoking one and that shocked her. She hadn't smoked in 10 years. She couldn't. She shouldn't. But she couldn't stop thinking about it. She put it out of her mind and then a cigarette butt was thrown from a passing car right in front of her, sparking on the ground. She reached over, grabbed the pack and slid one out. She rushed it to her lips before she changed her mind. Before she could think too much more about it, she lit it and inhaled. A sense of calm swarmed over her. And the ride was a little easier now.

The remainder of the ride was uneventful and she arrived at Jake's condo about the time she expected. She slid the gym bag over to her but still out of view of the windows. She grabbed the gun and held it in her hand for a minute. It made her feel safer. She removed the clip, added the bullets and put it back in the bag.

Lauren grabbed her purse and slung it over her shoulder. She grabbed the gym bag and watched the gun fall to the bottom of the bag, followed by the cigarettes. She thought of having another one but decided it wasn't as good as she thought. Tasted like she chewed on some dirty corduroys like the ones Creepy Carl wore.

She placed the gym bag on her hood, reached in and took off the safety and held the gun inside the bag. She locked her car twice just to be sure.

Lauren peered around as she walked to the entranceway to see if anyone was watching. She cupped her hand around the keypad and entered the code. This time she took the elevator to Jake's second floor condo. No more walking up the stairs today.

She opened the door, flicked the lights on and slammed the door shut. She made sure the knob was locked and then slid the deadbolt. She placed the gym bag on the couch and pulled out the gun. Then she flung her purse on the couch.

Lauren went room to room with the gun pointed in front of her, ready to shoot at anything that moved. She imitated every cop show she ever saw when they move from room to room to make sure it was clear. She felt like a bad ass when she searched, but truth is she was afraid. Once she cleared the rooms, she felt safer, but still afraid. Having Jake there would be better.

Standing there in the living room with the gun in her hand, she decided to check the fridge because she was not getting her fancy margarita tonight. She scavenged and found boxed wine left over from her visit to Jake the previous Saturday night. There was maybe enough for two glasses. That would have to do, she thought. Two for me; zero for Jake.

She noticed a block of cheese was left in the drawer. She grabbed it, but noticed a spot of mold on it. She turned up her nose but then thought "screw it." She grabbed the big knife from the wood block and cut off the mold. She poured the wine and took the cheese and crackers to the couch. And the gun came with her. That was her best friend right now.

Sitting on the couch drinking the wine made her feel better. She had stretched her legs along the couch. She still wanted Jake. But it would still be another 15 minutes at least. She gulped the last bit of wine from the glass. It wasn't too lady like, but she didn't care. She earned it after all this.

She leaned her head back on the couch and closed her eyes. She reached out for the gun and wrapped her hand around it the handle. Her maroon nails provided stark contrast to the grey gunmetal color of the weapon. She felt like a Femme Fatal from some movie. She pined for Jake who was now overdue.

Jake was sitting in his car on the side of the highway and blue lights from behind illuminated the interior of his car. The tap on the window was next. He moved his hands from the top of the steering wheel and lowered the window.

"You trying to break Chuck Yeager's land record pal?" asked the female officer.

"Officer, my girlfriend--," Jake began when he was interrupted by the officer with the standard license and registration demand. He got them both for her and tried one more time.

"Officer, please," he said. "I think my girlfriend is in danger. She thinks a guy is stalking her and she may be right."

The officer stared at him for a moment, trying to gauge if this was some sort of a ruse to get out of the ticket. But it would have to be good to explain going 85 mph on a medium crowded highway.

"I've been telling her for weeks it was in her head," he continued. "But he kept running into her on purpose. He moved her car today and offered her a ride."

The officer continued to read Jake and concluded he was genuine. 'Where is she now?" she asked.

"My condo," he said. "I sent her there because we were afraid that he knew her address."

The officer felt it all made sense, but that didn't get him out of the ticket.

"Tell you what I'm going to do," she began. "I'm going to call the local police where you live. Is this your correct address on the license?"

Jake shook his head yes.

"Okay. They will go check on her and will wait there until you arrive. I'm still writing you the ticket. After I let you go, you will drive the speed limit to her. Got it?"

Jake again shook his head yes and the officer walked away to write the ticket.

Meanwhile, Lauren started to drift off but jerked herself awake. She opened her eyes, sat up and kicked off her heels. She walked halfway to the kitchen and realized she left the gun on the couch. She shrugged and walked to the fridge.

She opened the door, leaned in and grabbed the box of wine. She closed the door, turned and standing in front of her was Creepy Carl. She started to breath heavy and dropped the wine on the floor. Her mouth was open. She couldn't believe it. Creepy Carl sneaked up on her again.

Tell me I'm asleep and this is a bad dream, she thought.

Carl stood there with his arms motionlessly hanging straight down against his grey corduroys. She couldn't see his hands because she didn't look down. He slowly raised his left hand. Lauren's eyes widened as his hand came into view. This time it was not a very thin clasp envelope. It was the big knife she had used to cut the block of cheese.

It seemed like an eternity and then he pursed his lips to speak. And then he finally spoke in his typical monotone voice.

"Mail call," he said.

Lauren screamed as he thrust the knife into the right side of her abdomen. Her scream was cut short by the searing pain that coursed through her body. Seconds later she felt her warm blood flowing onto her skin. It stained her new pink blouse and grey skirt. She felt the blood go under her skirt, over and under her stockings.

She reached out her hands to keep from falling and grabbed Creepy Carl's arms. She gasped and choked on blood that had filled her mouth. He reached out and grabbed her under her armpits with his thumbs pressed against her breasts. He slowly lowered her to the floor, pushing her arms off of him.

Lauren grunted and whimpered as she felt herself being lowered to the floor. She was in shock and the whole time her mind raced to try to figure out why this was happening. It's not a bad dream. She never thought Creepy Carl was capable of this but here they were. She was dying. He was killing her. Nobody was going to save her.

He laid her on the floor, fondled her breasts, grabbed the handle of the knife and pushed it deeper. Lauren shrieked. Creepy Carl yanked the knife out of her. She cried and moaned, feeling her own blood flowing out of her quicker now. Her mind was failing her. She couldn't feel her legs.

"Why?" she muttered.

He said nothing. Her breathing had become short and erratic. He just smiled at her the same way he did all the time at the office.

"Creepy Carl is watching you die, Lauren," he said.

Her eyes widened as she realized he knew her nickname for him. She coughed and tasted blood in her mouth. The last image she would see was Creepy Carl. With her last breath, she uttered, "Jake", closed her eyes, turned her head to the side. Lauren was no more.

There was a sudden bang on the door. "Open up. Police"

Lauren opened her eyes.

There was a louder bang on the door. "Open up. Police"

Lauren looked around. She was sitting on the couch. The gun was right next to her. She jumped up and screamed. It was a dream, she thought. It was a dream. She buried her face in her hands and tried to shake off the horror that she just went through.

"Open up. Police"

Lauren pushed herself up from the couch and nearly tripped over her heels that she flicked off her feet earlier.

"I'm coming," she yelled.

The door burst open and she turned to toward the police and screamed again. Their guns were pointed at her and she put her hands up. She was terrified but happy to be alive. The officers came in and immediately started going through the condo as she did earlier. She let them do their job and just stood there.

"Gun!" shouted one of the officers. "It's on the couch."

Lauren watched the police walk past her each scanning different areas of the condo.

"I got a body!" shouted the other officer, who walked into the kitchen and knelt down. The other officer stole a few glances but kept alert. Lauren could see the officer in the kitchen shaking his head back and forth. He was signaling that the person in the kitchen was dead.

The officers moved on to search the rest of the condo. A perplexed Lauren slowly walked to the kitchen. She had no idea what was happening. What body? Did she shoot and kill Creepy Carl and then fall asleep?

As she passed the breakfast nook at the end of the counter, she looked to the floor and saw a pair of feet covered in nylon stockings. She noticed the maroon red paint on the toe nails. She inched closer and saw a grey skater skirt and then a pink blouse. She looked at the face and it was her.

She saw herself lying still on the floor. The officer pronounced her dead. Her skirt and blouse were soaked in her own blood. A small trail of blood had dripped down her nylons past her kneecap and to her ankle.

That's me, she thought.

She tore her eyes away and looked at her abdomen. There was blood on her blouse, skirt and nylons, but she didn't feel any pain. The knife she used to cut the cheese was on the counter with blood all over it.

She looked back down at the kitchen floor and she was there too. Blood in exactly the same spots on her clothes. Her mind raced trying to sort this out.

If I am dead, why am I alive too? she questioned. This must be a dream.

Her analytical mind was working overtime, trying to comprehend what she was seeing in front of her. She went over to the officers.

"Am I dead?" she asked. "Hey you. What's going on? Am I dead?

The officers never addressed me, she thought. It's like I'm not here, but I am here.

Then it finally hit her. "Am I a ghost?"

"Hey you," she said to the officer closest to her. "Am I a ghost?"

There was no answer from him. He called in the homicide to police headquarters.

"Carl did this to me," she told him. "Creepy Carl. He is the mailroom guy at Liberty Square Financial."

But there was no response. She couldn't tell them anything. Hopefully they figure it all out.

She looked down on the floor again. There was a slight splatter of blood on her throat, under her chin. The makeup on her face was perfect as well as her berry lips and black eyelashes. Her eyes were closed putting her brown eye shadow on full display. Her terracotta brown hair was trapped under her shoulders and framed her face. Her double heart drop earrings laid on the floor next to her hair.

Lauren looked at herself laying on the floor, causing reality to set in. She started to cry. She walked away and sat on the couch.

"It's over," she thought. "I'm dead."

She cried a whole lot more.

ONE WEEK LATER

Jake was sitting on the couch in his condo. He was quiet and pensive. It was the first time he was back in his condo after the police had given him permission. The police had wrapped up their investigation and Lauren's body had been released earlier in the week. Jake was considered a person of interest but they cleared him because he had a solid alibi. He was getting a speeding ticket.

The wake was earlier in the week. The funeral was next day.

Now Jake just sat there distressed. Lauren was next to him but he didn't know it. She cuddled up against him like a puppy for want of attention. She also tried to console him for she saw the anguish on his face.

There was a rattle at the door. The sound of a key being inserted into the lock. It opened and a woman walked in. Jake got up as she shut the door. They looked at each other for a few seconds and then raced toward each other, embracing and kissing like it was a high school prom.

Lauren watched with her mouth agape. She couldn't believe what she was seeing. As she processed it, she realized Jake had to have been cheating on her. She got angrier every second she watched this spectacle.

Jake and the woman released each other.

"I need a drink," she said and walked toward the kitchen. She put her purse on the nook and started taking a bottle of wine out of the cloth bag she had in her hand.

"I'll have one too, Brenda," said Jake as he walked over toward her.

The two just gazed at each other and Lauren gazed at the both of them seething with rage.

"Is everything all set?" asked Brenda. "Is this going to work?"

"Absolutely," said Jake as he ran his hand up the side of her dress. "It's all arranged. I initialized the transfer orders just five minutes before they were due."

She smiled. He stepped behind her and brushed her blond hair from one shoulder to the other while kissing her on the neck. She cooed a bit and continued pouring the wine.

"Come over near the couch," she said as she gave him the sexy eyes. She walked over and he followed like a puppy. "You have the tickets?"

"Yeah," he said, pointing to the counter. "It's all set. The transfers are going through. I drained all of the foreign accounts that Lauren handled at the bank after I got the account numbers, passcodes and authorizations. The sweep accounts are automatic."

"And I have the passports," Brenda replied.

Brenda smiled. Jake smiled. Lauren's countenance was inexplicable. She was acrimonious as she realized that Jake used her to steal her clients' money and was cheating on her at the same time. She screamed, lunged at Jake and went right through him and the couch, landing on the floor.

"All that money will go the Grand Cayman accounts I set up," he continued. "We'll get there tonight. Tomorrow we'll walk in, get the money out and leave. Nobody figures it out until Monday morning. We'll be gone and in the clear."

"What about the guy who killed Lauren?" Brenda asked.

"Creepy Carl?" he chuckled. "I merely told that idiot I was going to pay him Monday for murdering Lauren."

They both howled with laughter. Lauren flew into a rage and tried to grab a lamp to throw at the two of them but she couldn't.

"How much?" Brenda asked as Lauren placed her hands on Brenda's neck to no avail.

"Thirty-eight million dollars," he said.

"AHHHHHHHHHHHHHHHHHHHHHHHH!!!!!!!!!!!!!!!" Lauren yelled in Jake's ear

"Did you hear something?" Jake asked.

Brenda shook her head no, smiled and raised her glass. Jake did the same. They clinked the glasses and then drank. Brenda drank a small sip. She then undid the top two buttons of her blouse and guzzled the rest of the wine. Jake got the hint. He guzzled his wine, put down the glass and started looking Brenda up and down.

He reached out for her but she had scooted onto the couch and laid there with her head on the arm rest. She raised her right leg and dangled her heel in front of him. He slipped off her heel and dropped it to the floor. He then did the same to the other one. She continued to undo the buttons of her blouse. He stood up and started to unloosen his belt. He started to lose his balance and caught himself. He smiled and then felt dizzy. His eyesight was suddenly a bit blurry.

"Am I drunk?" Jake thought.

"Finally," Brenda thought and she got up and started to button up her blouse.

Jake started choking and grabbed his abdomen. He was spitting up some blood.

Brenda reached down and grabbed her heels. "Not on my Louis Vuitton's you don't," she said as she stood back up and walked away.

Jake fell to his knees and looked at Brenda. He realized he was poisoned. He kept coughing and more blood came up. He was grabbing his stomach and choking.

"Hurry up," Brenda said. "I don't have all day. I've got a plane to catch."

Jake lurched forward, hitting his head on the coffee table and turning over on his back. He coughed a few more times and died, nestled between the couch and the coffee table.

Brenda walked over to her Gucci bag, grabbed a cigarette and lit it. Lauren was standing off in the corner watching this all transpire. She cheered and jumped up and down. She had revenge. She ran over to Jake's dead body and started yelling at him.

"How do you like it Jake? Huh? Huh? You have me murdered and you're cheating on me with this blond floozie too! Then she kills you. Ha! How does it feel idiot?"

As Brenda stood by the counter smoking and contemplated her actions, Lauren watched as Jake's ghost rose from his body. She continued to mock him. He rose to his feet and Lauren stood in front of him.

"Lauren?"

Lauren then smiled at him, wound up and slapped him across the face. But it still didn't work. Her hand went through Jake's face and she went forward, crashing through to the couch.

"Damn it!" she yelled. "I thought it would work that time. Do we get some sort of rule book?""

Jake was thoroughly confused.

"You're supposed to be dead," said Jake.

Lauren picked herself up and turned toward him.

"Yeah, it's me asshole! And I am dead."

"But why can I see you if you're dead?"

"Because you're dead too," she said as he felt his body from the chest down and looked at his body on the floor. "She poisoned you moron."

Jake turned and saw Brenda. He then looked down at his body on the floor. He looked at Lauren and back to Brenda. He felt his chest and then looked at his body on the floor again. He turned to Brenda.

"Bitch," he yelled as he lunged at her crashing into the wall.

Reality had set in for him. He screwed up. Brenda conned him. Lauren stood watching him put it all together and a smile burst across her face. Jake turned toward Lauren

"Lauren, honey," he began with his arms open like they were long lost friends who were meeting for the first time in years.

"Honey? You think that's going to work?"

"This wasn't my idea," he said. "It was Brenda's. I didn't want to have you killed. I just thought we could get away before you and the bank figured it out."

"So in the meantime you were just pretending to love me while you conned me?" she asked.

"Well, ah -" he responded as Lauren cut him off.

"And all the sex," she began. "Was that your idea or hers?"

"You know, I mean, you and I were a couple. If I didn't have sex with you, it would have been awkward."

"Awkward?" she yelled as she buried her upper lip with her bottom lip. "Awkward like right now."

Jake just rolled his eyes.

"Listen, it was all Brenda," he declared. "It was her idea to have you murdered."

"Sure," she said. "Blame the living."

"It's the truth," he pleaded. "She didn't want you talking to the police and perhaps helping them figure it out."

There was a rattle at the door. It opened and Creepy Carl walked in, gazing at Brenda with that look reserved only for lovers.

"It's all set," Brenda said. "The transfers are on their way. I've got the tickets and the fake passports with our pictures."

Creepy Carl looked at Jake's body on the floor. It was the second time he has seen a dead body in this condo. Jake and Lauren stood off to the side, just completely stunned. Brenda and Creepy Carl came together, clutching, grabbing and kissing each other like two teens in heat.

"You've got to be kidding me!" Jake exclaimed.

Lauren didn't know whether to laugh or cry as she watched the two of them. Part of her was astonished that Creepy Carl could get a woman with the looks of Brenda who had expensive tastes. But he was dressed rather dashing in a sports jacket, turtle neck and two-toned shoes.

"I'm rather gobsmacked that this bloody plan is going to work," he said in a British accent.

"Well, your acting was simply marvelous Creepy Carl," laughed Brenda.

Lauren realized that Creepy Carl was merely acting creepy and was dressing down. His hair was combed differently. He had on a nice pair of Brooks Brothers pants, a stylish Calvin Klein mock turtle neck sweater and nice pair of brown Florsheim shoes. And he had a British accent. He cleans up really nice, she thought. She was torn between liking and hating him. After a few seconds, she lunged at Carl but made no impact. Jake started to mock her.

Creepy Carl walked Brenda backward against the wall with a burst of passion. Brenda got weak in the knees as he slid has hand up to her breast. She put her head back against the wall and closed her eyes. Creepy Carl slid his hand up to her neck, wrapped his hand around it and squeezed. Brenda's eyes opened in time to see Creepy Carl's other hand reach for her neck. He began strangling her and Brenda gasped.

When Jake and Lauren realized that Creepy Carl was killing Brenda, they looked at each other with amazement. Jake then started cheering and jumping up and down.

Brenda tried to push Creepy Carl away but he was too strong. She tried to reach for something to hit him with but nothing. She started to feel a burning in her chest due to the lack of oxygen in her lungs. It took about three minutes for Creepy Carl to kill Brenda. She stared back at him the whole time and died with her eyes as wide as saucers. Creepy Carl gently laid Brenda down on the floor. Jake thought the expression on her face was priceless.

Creepy Carl gathered the tickets and the passports. He looked at Brenda and then at Jake. Two more dead bodies in this apartment for a total of three, he thought. The police are going to have a hell of a time figuring this one out.

Suddenly Brenda's ghost rose out of her body. She did the same thing as Jake. Got up, looked around and tried to figure it all out. Jake wasted no time. He went toward Brenda and wound up for a big slap.

"No, no, no," Lauren yelled. "It's not going to work."

Jake didn't listen and swung at Brenda, totally going through her and the counter and falling face first on the kitchen floor.

"What the hell was that?" Brenda yelled, looking at Lauren.

"Hi there! How does it feel to be dead?" asked Lauren very sarcastically.

Brenda looked at Lauren very inquisitively.

"You're dead," she said.

"So are you?" responded Lauren.

"I guess I am," said Brenda as she looked at her corpse. "Barnaby double crossed me."

"Barnaby," exclaimed Lauren. "His name is not even Carl."

"Sorry honey but no," explained Brenda. "He is an actor that got expelled by the acting community in England after he saved the King and killed MacBeth in the premiere at the Royal Opera House."

Jake had pulled himself off the floor and walked over.

"Remember me? I'm dead too because you poisoned me," said Jake.

"But he strangled me," Brenda shot back. "That was really painful. I couldn't breathe. My mouth was so dry and my lungs were burning. Poison was a simpler death for you."

"Are you kidding me?" Jake responded. "I started choking and spitting up blood. You think that was a piece of cake?"

"What the hell is wrong with the both of you? Creepy Carl stabbed me to death. That hurt a lot. And blood dripped all over one of my favorite skirts and my new pink blouse. Now I have to wear these bloody clothes for eternity."

"Where are your shoes?" Brenda asked Lauren.

"I had taken them off and went to the kitchen for more wine," she responded. "I guess when you die, your ghost wears what you wore at the time of your death."

"Shame," said Brenda. "I think we're the same size. I would let you borrow my Louis Vuittons."

"OMG!" exclaimed Lauren. "Those are gorgeous. I wish I could."

"What's going on with you two?" yelled Jake. "I mean, we've all been double crossed, and murdered while Creepy Carl is alive and well. What are we going to do about this?"

"What can we do?" asked Brenda as she tried to grab a cigarette to no avail. "Damn!"

"Yeah," echoed Lauren. "We're dead. We can't hit each other. We can't touch anything. How can we stop him?"

"He just gets away with it?" said Jake.

The three of them stood there all watching Creepy Carl finish gathering everything he needed. He took one more look at Brenda, went to the door and peeked out to make sure nobody was there. He opened it and closed it quick.

Creepy Carl was going to get away with murder and $38 million.

He was no longer Creepy Carl.

He was Brilliant Barnaby.

Voice from the Scary Side

C hristmas 1973. It was a haunted Christmas.

I was 12 years old and was so excited for Christmas just like any young boy my age. What was Santa Claus going to bring me? Would I get a new bike? Would my aunt give me yet another pair of tube socks?

It was Christmas Eve so school was only a half day. I raced home from the middle school that was just around the corner. I cut across the baseball and soccer fields to reach the brook, where I spent plenty of time hanging out with my friends on most days. But not today.

As I got to the edge of the brook, I leapt onto the first stone and carefully navigated the rest of them to reach the other side.

I quickly darted past the six-foot cement sewer cylinders that laid on their side, languishing in a deserted lot near my home. The cement sewer cylinders were a popular spot. They were large enough to sit in and do all sorts of things. The older kids would go there to smoke or drink.

And some even got intimate with each other. Many of us younger kids would carefully hide in the brush nearby and watch because we were curious. I once saw a local teenager in one of the cylinders with a girl who had her shirt off. I remember watching for several minutes until he spotted me yelled for me to go away.

But I had no time for that today despite my pre-pubescent curiosity. I was in that middle ground of being somewhat interested in girls and still believing in Santa Clause. And it was Christmas Eve. I needed to get home and prepare. The countdown had begun and I could not contain my excitement.

I darted across the street and bolted down the sidewalk, waving to the horse that was in a corral diagonally behind the old Beaton House. I was a latch key kid so I grabbed my key out of my pocket only to realize the door was unlocked because my mom was home. The car wasn't there. She had lent it to a friend.

I said "Hi" to my mom and then stopped in front of the Christmas tree that stood in the corner of the room in between the fireplace and the couch. It was a real tree; not one of those fake ones. There were only a handful of gifts under the three but I knew there would be more in the morning.

"Homework!" my mom yelled, breaking my stare.

I really didn't have much homework at all. A few teachers gave us some reading over school vacation, but many didn't because then they would have to grade it. Teachers need a vacation from us kids.

I went in my room and made off as though I was doing my homework, but I wasn't focused. I just sat there at my wooden desk that belonged to my dad and my grandfather. My books were open in front of me. I'd occasionally get up and walk around the room. Perhaps I'd fiddle with my models of aircraft carriers and airplanes.

It was all hurry up and wait. I didn't know what to do with myself. I'd come out of my room from time to time to examine dinner, open the fridge or steal a glance at the Christmas tree. My mom watched me pace around the house as she made dinner. She was probably chuckling to herself. I can't say I blame her.

My mom was old school so there was no way I was getting any gifts on Christmas Eve, even if I was an only child. I didn't even ask. She worked school hours in the shoe department of a major department store chain. She would go to the super market after work and then come to make dinner.

I watched the clock and the hours slowly passed. It seemed like an eternity. I swear the clock was going backwards some of the time.

My dad finally came home from work. He owned a hardware store around the corner. My dad was an engineer and was very handy. He could fix anything and sometimes it did not include duct tape. He was also in the military in WW2 so he wasn't afraid of anything.

Dinnertime finally arrived and I could barely eat. I honestly don't even remember what we had. And the hours droned on after dinner. There were some Christmas specials on television with lots of singing, dancing and joyous celebration. All that did was make me more excited.

My dad got tired of my antsy behavior and told me to go to my room or just go downstairs. I chose to go downstairs to the playroom. It was a room my dad had renovated with pine boards on the walls, a bar, built in bookcase and a pool table.

He had a sign on the playroom wall that read "Smile." When guests had a few drinks in them, he would turn the sign over and it would read "Snile." If they noticed, he'd tell them they had too much to drink.

I played a little pool but that got boring quickly. I threw some darts but didn't come close to the bull's eye. I finally spied the electronic organ. My mom bought it from my cousin because my aunt bought one. I'm pretty sure that my cousin got them because they fell off a truck.

I walked over, sat down and turned it on. I decided to sing Christmas songs. I was going to put all of my nervous energy to good use. I grabbed the song book, flipped the pages and found Jingle Bells. I couldn't read music, but all I had to do was press the numbered keys that corresponded to the numbers in the book.

It started off very slow. Jing … gle … Bells. Jing … gle … Bells. Jing … gle … all …the … way.

I got better at it after 20 minutes and it actually started to sound like Jingle Bells. It was going really well. The pacing and cadence were so much better. It actually seemed like I knew what I was doing. It never would have been good enough for Broadway, but I was into it.

And then I heard a voice. I stopped playing, craned my neck to the left to look at the stairs behind me. Nobody was there. I thought my mom or dad was calling me so I went over to the stairs and looked up. The door was closed. Nobody was there. Must have been something outside, I thought to myself.

I went back to the organ and started playing again. I started singing Jingle Bells again and heard a voice again after a few minutes.

I looked around the finished portion of the basement. Nobody was there. I checked the stairs and saw nobody.

There was one more place to check and that was the unfinished side of the basement, known as the scary side. I never went in there unless I absolutely had to. The finished side was safety. The unfinished side was not. The furnace, hot water tank, washer, dryer and oil tank were there.

Beyond the washer and dryer was the tool room area. That was the forbidden zone so I never went there. It's not that my parents told me not to, it's just that my bedroom was above that room. And when I went to bed for the night, I always felt that something might be in that room and come up and get me as I slept. No way was I going to stir anything up.

Despite all my fears, something drew me to the scary side on Christmas Eve. I heard a voice and wondered what or who it was. The light was off on the scary side so my mom was not there doing a load of laundry. There was no reason for me to go check, but for whatever reason, I summoned the courage and ventured in.

As I stepped over the threshold from safety to scary, I extended my right hand toward the light switch. It was a push button. All I had to do was press it. I kept one foot in the safe side of the basement as I reached as far as I could to hit the push button. It was as if I was a first baseman keeping my foot on the base while reaching out to catch the ball to make sure the runner was out.

I pushed the button, causing the light to turn on and illuminated the washer and dryer in front of me. The furnace was to my left. I slowly walked in ready to bolt if necessary. I peered out from the edge of the old metal kitchen cabinets that my dad installed. I saw nothing and then stepped out into the middle of the room, looking past the washer and dryer toward the forbidden zone that was underneath my bedroom.

Nothing.

Now I turned around and went the other way. I would have to walk past the furnace to get to the oil tank area. There was storage across from it. My mom would send me downstairs to get kitchen supplies that were stored there. I dreaded those moments and that is when I wished I had a brother or sister who would volunteer for such perilous duty.

What bothered me the most about that spot was the area under the stairs. No light shone there. It was the black hole of the basement. It was by far the most frightening area of the house. All you saw was darkness. I called it The Void. There could be a monster hiding under the stairs and you wouldn't see it, but it could see you.

The other significant part of the stairs that scared the wits out of me was the opening. There was about an eight-inch square opening between the stairs and the storage area. It was next to your feet as you went up the stairs. Whenever I walked up and down the stairs, I never walked next to the opening. I always went on the other side of the stairs. You didn't know what was there because it was pitch black.

My dad knew that I was afraid of the opening. Earlier that year, my dad was downstairs one day when I was going up the stairs. As I got toward the opening, he reached out, grabbing my leg. I screamed like a distressed hyena. I couldn't jump a mile because my dad was holding my leg. He finally let go of my leg and I reached the top of the stairs to find my mother standing there.

"What the hell is going on?" demanded my mom, who would punish my cousins and I when we acted up by putting us in the corner. I often wished I lived in a circular home so there were no corners. Then what would she do?

I looked at my mom, babbled something and walked away until I recovered.

I had screamed like that a year earlier at my cousin's home. We were on the porch watching TV. My parents, aunts and uncles were in the next room playing cards. I was laying down in a very awkward manner for quite some time. The show was over so I got up and was then struck by a debilitating muscle cramp. I played hockey as a kid and got these cramps regularly. This one was excruciating, and I let out a scream as loud as sasquatch and fell to the floor.

My mom entered the room. "Stop fooling around!" she said before turning around to leave. Meanwhile, I was writhing on the floor in pain. I was in sheer agony and she left me there on the floor. My cousins did nothing either; they might have laughed.

I was afraid that the third banshee scream of my life was upon me as I approached the void under the stairs. I was standing on the cusp of the darkness. My eyes adjusted to the low light as the opening was just above my head. I could see the wall three feet away now. There was nothing there.

I was scared but relieved. It still didn't explain the voice, but I felt comfortable that nobody was in the basement. I went back to the safety of the finished playroom to resume playing the organ.

I settled in and began to play Jingle Bells for the 37th time. It was going really well now. I had rhythm and pace. I was feeling it. I was in the Christmas spirit. Everything was going great. For a few minutes, I was the world's greatest showman.

And then it happened.

For the third time, I heard a voice. It was not muffled like before. It was loud and it was clear.

"You're not supposed to sing, stupid," said the disembodied voice.

I stopped singing. I froze like a statue. I could not move for 30 seconds. I did not know what to do. Was it behind me? Was it to my left? My right? Or was it on the scary side? Yeah. Must be on the scary side.

I had to get the hell out of there, but I couldn't leave on the organ or lights because I would get in trouble even if some sort of monster was about to kill me. I slowly reached over and turned off the switch on the organ. I slowly turned, got off the bench and surveyed the room. You see, it is much safer to move slowly then whatever is there isn't sure what you are going to do. But I knew exactly what I was going to do.

I waited about five seconds and then bolted. I stuck out my left hand, aiming for the light switch on the wall next to the stairs. I hit all three push buttons at the same time with the palm of my hand to shut off the playroom lights.

At the same time, I had stretched out my right leg toward the stairs, landing on the second step. The jump was worthy of Olympic quality. I took two steps at a time, ascending to the first floor quicker than ever.

When I reached the top of the stairs, I swung the door open like Kramer entering Jerry Seinfeld's apartment. My parents were sitting at the kitchen table. They looked at me and I was terrified.

"You look like you've seen a ghost," my dad commented.

I shook my head in agreement and then started babbling incessantly about voices in the basement.

"The house is haunted!" I screamed. "We got to leave!"

I was jumping up and down, ranting and raving and was completely inconsolable. My mom tried to calm me down, while my dad ordered me to knock it off.

"There's nothing downstairs," he exclaimed.

"Ghost. Ghost! GHOST!!!!!!" I yelled.

It took a few minutes before I finally caught my breath and started to calm down. I explained what happened and my dad told me it was my imagination. I asked him to go down and check and he said no. As I began to get riled up again, I heard those words that every parent speaks at one time or another.

"Go to your room," he began, "And don't come out."

Go to my room? My room was above the forbidden zone in the basement. That can't be good. But I didn't argue. I was glad to do it. I decided that I would stay in my room above the Forbidden Zone under my covers cowering in fear where it is safe.

Everyone knows that when you are under the covers, the ghosts, demons and monsters cannot find or hurt you. I didn't move from that spot. I was still terrified because there was something in the basement.

It was Christmas Eve and I was one of many 12-year-olds who couldn't fall asleep. But most of the others were so excited for Christmas Day that they couldn't fall asleep. Me? I couldn't fall asleep because I was scared beyond belief that there was something in the basement. And nobody believed me.

The morning came and I was still in my bed and under the covers. It was well after 8 am. I usually woke my parents up on Christmas hours earlier, dragging them to the living room to open gifts. This was the first time that my parents had to come get me.

They stood at my bedroom door, encouraging me to come to the living room. I sat up in the bed, holding the covers to my chin and shook my head no.

"What's wrong?" my mom asked. "Don't you want your gifts?"

I looked at her and muttered words to the effect that there was a ghost downstairs.

"That's it!" my dad bellowed. "This ends right now. Get out of that bed and come with me."

My fate had arrived. My dad ordered me to go down stairs with him so he could prove there was nothing down there. But I knew the truth. I followed behind him down the hall, through the living room and the kitchen to get to the basement stairs. I was about six feet behind him, moping and whimpering.

We descended the stairs and I moved away from the opening as usual. I figured that whatever was in the basement would get him first and I may be able to get away. I thought that my dad should be wearing one of those red Star Trek shirts because those guys always got killed when they beamed down to the planet with Capt. Kirk.

We entered the playroom first. My dad switched on the lights and scanned the room. I stood behind him the whole time. There was nothing so we moved on. We were now heading to the scary side of the basement. I was certain that this was where the ghost was hiding.

My dad strolled into the room without a care in the world. He switched on the lights and there was the washer and dryer. The tool room was to the side just as before and nothing was out of place.

He walked toward the furnace and I followed. There was nothing out of place. Now the moment of truth had arrived. We had to walk over to The Void. I was certain this would be the end. My dad walked over, looked under the stairs and peered into the darkness. Nothing.

"See?" he said. "There is nothing here."

"But Dad," I argued, "The voice told me to stop singing."

My dad had a quizzical look on his face. Apparently, I hadn't mentioned that before when I hysterically described what happened.

He ushered me over to the electronic organ. We looked each other in the eye as if to make sure we were both ready. He turned on the organ without looking. We both looked at the organ.

"What were you playing?" he asked.

I pointed to Jingle Bells that was still left open on the top of the organ.

My dad had worked as a communications lineman when he was in WW2. He was also an engineer. He was familiar with electronics and clearly was part detective. He had an idea what was going on. I was clueless partly because I was still afraid and also because I was 12-years-old.

He started to press some of the keys. A few minutes had passed and there was nothing. Now he started speaking as he pressed the keys. Still nothing. Finally, he struck a pair of keys at the same time and spoke.

"Is there a ghost here?" he asked

There was static and then suddenly a voice burst through.

"There's no ghosts here," they exclaimed. "We're just having fun on Christmas. Over."

I stepped backward and crashed into the pool table as my dad continued to press keys and talk.

"Who are you?" my dad asked. "Over."

It turns out they were our neighbors across the street. They just got a CB Base Radio for Christmas. The antenna wasn't matched properly so they were splashing over anything electronic. My dad and I talked to our neighbors across the street for close to an hour.

I was relieved. It wasn't a ghost. It was our neighbors. The house wasn't haunted after all.

And the reason why they said, "You're not supposed to sing stupid" is because FCC regulations do not allow singing on CB band radio.

My dad figured that striking keys in a certain order created a certain frequency that was able to receive the neighbors when they transmitted. He wasn't sure how we were transmitting, but assumed we were simply piggybacking on the same frequency.

All I remember is that Christmas 1973 was a haunted Christmas and I don't even recall what I got for gifts that year

For the next Christmas, I asked my parents for a CB radio.

CREAM PUFFS AND
A MADMAN

It was one of those brisk autumn evenings that send tingling messages through the spine. A night which would be dark and dreary even with the light of a full moon. It was the type of night beat cops dread to patrol, especially the skeleton shift.

However, duty always prevailed and O'Malley got the call. His patrol would take him through Scollay Square, the outskirts of the common and the north slope of Beacon Hill.

The patrol would not be consumed with danger, but O'Malley would see with his own eyes the work of the devil and his hellions (as he believed it).

O'Malley was dressed mostly from head to toe in blue. The buttons of his frock coat were in their proper place down the middle, keeping it snug about him. The flare of the frock coat extended past his gluteus maximus. His pants were bulging at the thighs, for on such a night, one wore extra garments to keep warm.

The wide black belt latched in the front holding the frock coat in place. It was his belt of security, but there would be nothing on that belt that could help him, unless it contained silver bullets, a wooden stake, a mallet, garlic cloves and a cross. He wouldn't need the cross on his belt for he wore it around his neck.

His shoes were polished black and were tight on his feet as he wore two pairs of socks. Though the disadvantage of this was that he had to pull one sock up all the time since his garter only held one up. He wore no gloves, but he did wear a custodian helmet that would be swept off his head when the wind howled even though the strap was secured under his chin.

Before the night was over, he would grasp his gun and aim at a target that would not be human or at least appear not to be. Fear would wrap arms with O'Malley and let go only when it felt it had done its job on him.

The night seemed to drag so O'Malley played his usual games to keep himself occupied and alert. After passing through Scollay Square and tipping his hat to the evening ladies, he trekked down Tremont Street and stopped at the Granary Burying Grounds. He took his hat off his head and said a little prayer for old Mister Hodges who was buried there the day before. No one survived the honest and trusted haberdasher. There was nobody to take over the shop. The city auctioned most of his goods and used the funds to pay for the burial. Any excess money was put to a fund to maintain his grave going forward.

Despite his respect for Hodges, O'Malley would say a prayer from the sidewalk. After all, who was foolish enough to go into a graveyard on Halloween night? O'Malley certainly wasn't, that's for certain.

As he walked on, O'Malley began to whistle. He stopped as he turned the corner at the Boston Common to head toward the new statehouse that was built only 18 years ago. A fine building it was, he thought.

He looked over the statehouse from that distance and remembered the day it was announced that such a building was planned. He was young then, just 26 years old.

This served to take his mind off the night for only a short time. The second he turned toward the Boston Common his fears came back and he began to whistle even louder.

He wasn't afraid of the various robbers and thieves that waylayed in the shadows for an unsuspecting person to cross their path, he was afraid of the darkness. He was afraid of the unknown. Peering into the dark vestiges of the common made him somewhat discombobulated and his mind raced.

It had been a fortnight since he had to run into the Boston Common to chase down a thief, who stole a pocket watch and handbag from a young couple. He got to the middle and lost the thief partly because he was too slow and partly because the darkness got to him.

He found himself next to the location of the Great Elm that had been used to hang criminals since the 1600s. The tree had come down in a storm back some 30 years earlier, but it still was a source of anxiety, causing him trepidation.

The last hanging was 1817 but had heard tales that the spirits of the executed lingered there. He had heard that a few convicted witches were reportedly hanged there too. Some people claimed to have seen the bodies hanging from the trees on the anniversaries of the executions. He found this unsettling to say the least and downright upsetting to say the most.

In addition, he knew the British army had bivouacked there during the Revolutionary War. And the Central Burying Ground on the far side of the common next to Boylston Street interred British common soldiers, who died in combat or of disease as well as patriots from the battle of Bunker Hill. Reportedly, Boston Tea Party members were there too.

All these memories rushed more and more to the forefront of his mind and he whistled even louder. He got that feeling you get when you are alone at that late hour of the night with an ocean of seemingly endless black on one side of them and numerous dark alleys on the other. Someone was watching him he thought. Someone was going to jump him from the alley.

Fear was such a part of him now that he cautioned himself as he neared the first alley. He hugged the wall with his back and inched toward the corner of the building to try and take whatever was there by surprise. He then prepared to turn and stare into the darkness and see what was there, perhaps drawing his gun if necessary.

On the count of three, he turned into the alley with his hand on his gun and there was nothing. He realized he was being childish so he turned to leave the alley.

As he turned, he saw something move near his feet. It was small and ran right over his foot. He then saw a something bigger lurch toward his foot. His glance caught the yellowish eyes of the bigger creature, the red tongue and the fangs. It was a black cat that pounced on a rat and got it between O'Malley's feet. He saw the red eyes of the rat beaming in the darkness as the cat clutched it in its claws.

The adroit quickness of the cat caught him by surprise and he jumped backward hoping not to be clawed. He fell back into the trash cans and landed on the ground. The cat played with the rat that briefly escaped the cat by crawling on O'Malley.

The cat then pounced again onto him and snagged the rat again. He struggled to get up and was yelling as loud as he could as the cat and rat were fighting on top of him.

O'Malley rolled over the cat that dragged its prey off of him. He scrambled to the end of the alley on all fours, got up and brushed himself off. He looked back to see the cat holding the rat that was still alive. The cat hissed and the rat looked at O'Malley as if to ask for help.

"You're on your own pal," he said aloud.

He watched the cat play with its meal for a minute. The cat hissed at O'Malley and he took his cue to leave.

As he started to walk away, he realized he was more frightened of the odd thoughts he was having than the actual cat and the rat. He was letting his imagination run away with every sound he heard.

He heard a laugh and saw an old woman looking out a window. She apparently saw the whole disparaging escapade. She looked at O'Malley and bellowed. Not a laughing matter he thought. He ripped his shirt and his wife would give him quite the earful for it. He couldn't afford another shirt on his patrolman's salary of $12 a week. She would have to mend it.

O'Malley began to walk up the hill again and cared not to look at the dark Boston Common. He could see the gaslights in the distance, but they were far and few between to illuminate the mystery between them.

As he walked, he heard strange sounds again, but these sounded different. It started with a footstep, then a second later another and then very quickly there would be a striking of something hollow. The pattern kept repeating.

He pulled out his timepiece and noted the time as a quarter past eleven. Odd time, he thought, for someone to be out walking, except, of course, for a beat cop.

The proximity of the sound was near so he decided to stop, and as he did, the sound stopped. He became very suspicious and was not certain that his intuition was correct. He was being watched, but by whom?

O'Malley turned around as swiftly as he could, but saw and empty street. He glanced toward the common and saw nobody. He turned and looked in all directions trying to uncover anything improper that he could use to justify in his mind that he was not going crazy. He was confounded and began to question his own sanity.

He shrugged his shoulders and walked on figuring whatever was going to happen was going to happen and he should only prepare for it instead of worrying about it.

Well, whatever was going to happen had begun. He heard a sound. This time it was as real as it gets. It was clear as the tintinnabulation of a bell. It was the sound of an engine of a motor car.

He turned around to see a Model T making its way up the street. The driver had had his fill of liquor, he thought, since the car was going from side to side and occasionally striking the fence that separated the street from the common. Yet, it still roared up the hill dents and all. He could hear the driver screaming for help. No, he realized, that was not a cry for help. That was a laugh. The laugh of a madman.

He watched as the motor car crashed into a post. The driver lay over the steering wheel and was motionless. O'Malley inched closer to see who it was. When he was just 20 feet away, the driver looked up and glared at O'Malley, who froze in his tracks. They each looked at each other and then the driver let out a rather boisterous laugh.

It was then that O'Malley realized that the driver was none other than Theodore Lowell Adams the third, who was president of a prominent and elite Gentlemen's Club. He was a very respectable man and O'Malley was stunned to witness Adams acting this way.

On the sight of O'Malley, Adams started the engine, reversed the motor car from the post, put the gears in forward with an awful grinding sound and headed for O'Malley as fast as the Model T could go.

O'Malley ran for his life up the hill with Adams' Model T in pursuit. Had he been able to run this fast a fortnight ago, he would have caught that thief, he thought. As O'Malley ran to the right, Adams directed the motor car to the right and then followed him to the left.

A frantic O'Malley saw a broken section of the Boston Common fence and jumped into it. The ground was uneven and he lost his balance tumbling into the darkness of the Boston Common. The Model T sped away but O'Malley got up and instinctively kept running, fearing that the driver was still coming at him. He finally stopped to catch his breath and realized he was about 100 feet into the common, surrounded by the darkness. He was safe for the moment.

"Pick your poison," he mumbled as he awkwardly felt safe despite being on the common that he dreaded.

O'Malley slowly turned to face the rest of the Boston Common. He couldn't see anything but was completely spooked. He kept turning around as he walked away, constantly checking to make sure nothing was behind him. He did this until he got to the street and then took a rest.

The Chief-of-Police was not going to believe this, he thought. Maybe he shouldn't mention it at all for fear of being ridiculed. As he finally calmed down and regained his composure, he decided it would be best not to mention the common or his dealings with the cat and the rat, but he was determined to question Adams and perhaps arrest him for attempted murder.

O'Malley began to walk in the direction that Adams drove the Model T. He made sure to give himself an escape route in case the madman came back at him. He slowly made his way down sidewalks, around buildings and in the area of Beacon Hill. He had a pretty good idea that Adams was heading to the Gentleman's Club.

He finally arrived at the club, and saw Adams' Model T parked out front. The door was open. It had been ripped off its hinges. O'Malley questioned if he wanted to pursue the matter since the door was in splinters. He wanted answers so he approached with extreme caution and one hand on his gun that remained holstered for now.

As he entered the building, he looked around trying to spot anything out of place and clues to the direction that Adams took. He noticed that all the plaques were in the same spot they have always been. None were missing. He started up the stairs to go to the second-floor offices but heard a clash of metal pots in the kitchen, which was in the basement.

He ventured down to the kitchen and sure enough found Adams, who was grinning ear to ear like a gigglemug as he opened cabinets and drawers. He was looking for something, but what. O'Malley settled in at the door and watched for a minute before taking action.

What he was about to see was some of the most erratic behavior he had ever seen. In his 20 years walking the beat, he had never seen anything like it.

Adams ran around the room screaming and laughing, unbeknownst that he was being watched. He threw pots into the wall and occasionally ran into the wall as his grins and smiles turned to hysterical laughing.

He was mad, O'Malley thought. The man he knew was acting like he should be confined to an asylum for observation and restrained for his own safety. He was out of his mind and, perhaps, out of his body. This couldn't be Adams, he mused, but it was him in the flesh.

O'Malley tried to justify what he was witnessing. This couldn't be Adams. Something must have taken him over. He's a man of refined taste. He's a gentleman and a man of culture. But what he watched was nothing of the sort. He must be possessed by the devil. He was acting evil. He was a madman.

Suddenly, Adams stopped. He had spotted what he was looking for. He went over and grabbed a plate of cream puffs. He ate the first one by stuffing it entirely in his mouth. He ate another and another. He was consuming the cream puffs like a wild animal.

Adams then jumped up on the counter and started dancing. O'Malley ducked away from the door way as Adams twirled around and around, constantly releasing his insane laugh that would echo in the hallways outside the kitchen. O'Malley was getting used to that laugh now.

The madman jumped off the table and ran into the wall a few more times. O'Malley watched nervously and started to shake. He moved slightly and Adams stopped just before picking up another cream puff. O'Malley prayed Adams did not see him.

Adams went wild again. He crashed into the table, pretending he could run through it. He ran to the knife rack and pulled out the cleaver. He looked it over by bringing it inches to his face and then smiled so he could see his reflection in the stainless steel. He had returned to being a gigglemug.

He ran his finger along the edge and cut himself and began to bleed a little. He screamed at the sight of his own blood and then raised the cleaver as high as he could and brought it down on the wooden counter again and again and again.

O'Malley had crept back into the doorway for a better view and saw that the cleaver was wedged into the counter and appeared stuck.

Adams ate some more cream puffs and then glanced at the cleaver. He stared at it for what seemed to be forever. Adams smirked and O'Malley realized why. He was visible in the reflection of the cleaver. Adams saw him but O'Malley felt that Adams knew he was there all along.

O'Malley watched as Adams used both his hands to rip the cleaver out from the wood. He raised it inches away from his throat and drew it as if he has going to kill himself. Instead, he turned around, looked directly at O'Malley and pointed the cleaver at him while donning an impish grin.

They stared at each other with an awkward silence. Finally, O'Malley decided to step out from the doorway and try to reason with the madman.

"Okay there, Mr. Adams," he began. "It's time to go home. You've certainly done enough hell raisin' for the night. Put down the cleaver and let me take you home."

Adams' impish grin slowly turned to an angry sneer. He screamed as if this ritual was not meant for outsiders. He hovered over the cream puffs as if he was a mother protecting her children.

He then jumped up on the counter with cat like reflexes. From a crouched position, he kept screaming and screaming while still clutching the cleaver.

O'Malley finally drew his gun for he feared Adams was going to lunge at him. The madman's answer to this tense standoff was to drop the cleaver, grab the cream puffs and start throwing them at O'Malley.

The cream puffs came rapid fire and O'Malley was taken by

surprise. He was struck in the face, the chest and the arm. One knocked his hat off his head. The flummoxed O'Malley dropped his gun and Adams took the opportunity to run out of the room while carrying the remaining cream puffs.

O'Malley wiped the cream from his faces and eyes and reached for his gun a few times before finally grasping it. He heard Adams laughing as he went up the stairs. It was a sound he would never forget.

He charged up the stairs and raced out the front door but Adams was gone. The Model T was gone. The doors were no longer in splinters. O'Malley questioned his own reality.

What had happened? Was this real? Did he dream this?

He strolled over to a window that acted as a mirror. He looked at himself and there were no remnants of any cream puffs on his uniform.

He began to chuckle to himself. Then he chuckled out loud. He broke into a full laugh that became eerily similar to Adams' laugh that he heard all night. And then he caught a reflection of himself in the window. But it wasn't him. It was Adams.

O'Malley turned around but Adams was nowhere to be found. He gazed into the window once more and saw Adams. And then he realized that he was Adams all along.

∞∞∞∞∞

I wrote this story when I was in college in 1981, working for the school newspaper. We needed a Halloween story and I wrote this piece the night before the morning deadline. I had stumbled across an article involving a mock trial against a well-respected individual of a prominent association. I decided to create a spooky story around it. I have re-imagined the story over 40 years later.

STARING INTO THE DARKNESS

Frank kept checking his GPS as he meandered his way down the interstate highway that cut through a seemingly endless forest. The road curved around dense pockets of rock that the highway workers had been unable to blast through all those years ago. It was a nice drive, albeit long, especially coming all the way from New Jersey.

The scenery was nice, especially when it opened up to a view. It was breathtaking. It was vastly different than the deserts he had been in when he served in the Air Force at Ali al-Salem AFB in Kuwait. He had been transferred to McGuire AFB for the last year of his tour of duty and was discharged only a week ago. It was the perfect time to visit his friend up in Maine.

It was a bit of a drive for him but he was okay with it. He wasn't an antsy type of person and did not get rattled by much of anything whether it was gunfire, loud booms or long periods of time where he was confined to a small space. The military had trained him well. Nothing seemed to bother him. He was mentally tough.

He cranked some tunes and enjoyed the ride as he made his way through the beautiful vistas that made up this wonderful state. And he passed many farms, some of which he smelled before he saw them. The GPS instructed him to get off the highway onto an old state road. After driving a few miles, he thought he saw a couple of black and white cows crossing the road in the distance. He slowed down and stopped to let them pass. When he got up to the animals, he realized they were horses and not cows.

"Franky's cows are horses," he chuckled to himself, thinking that he should make an appointment to get his eyes checked when he returned home.

His GPS beeped and he knew he was close. A few minutes later, he was arriving at his friend's home. Situated a few miles northwest of Portland in a town called Cumberland, he drove down a gravel road to a beautiful Victorian style house that was typical of a Queen Anne style but had gothic revival overtones. A gigantic turret ran from the first floor to the attic.

It was ornate in that it was a mixture of conflicting styles that somehow fit together when you wouldn't expect them too. A wrap around porch embraced the front and sides. The house stood out amongst the landscape that had a big field next to it. It was a far cry from the barracks. He was happy that his friend was able to own such a beautiful home.

It was mid-afternoon as he pulled in the driveway. Bob came running out of the house as soon as he noticed Frank coming up the driveway. His wife, Susan, trailed behind him. The pair of military buddies practically jumped into each other's arms as Susan watched while wearing a big smile.

"Frank," said Bob as he stepped back, "I'd like you to meet my wife, Susan."

Susan stepped forward and extended her hand. "It's so nice to meet you," she said.

Frank extended his hand, grabbed hers and pulled her in for a hug as her husband laughed. When he finally let her go, he took a good long look at the house.

"Beautiful home," said Frank. "Clearly, the Air Force was paying you way more than me."

"Not really," laughed Bob. "It wasn't too expensive because it was a fixer upper. I still have work to do on it, but it's livable for now."

They went into the house and Bob started to explain the ski conditions on the slopes that were extremely favorable.

Susan brought Frank up to his room that was down a narrow hallway at the top of the stairs on the second floor. It was a small room that was barely big enough for a twin bed. There was a tiny built-in bureau, some hooks on the wall, a lamp on a table and a tiny square window that had a crank on it. There was barely enough room for Frank to put down his bag.

"It's cozy," Susan chimed. 'We're still working on the other bedrooms."

"This is luxury compared to sleeping quarters at McGuire," Frank explained as he began to put some of his clothes in a built-in bureau.

"I'll go downstairs and make coffee for all of us," Susan said as she excused herself out of the room.

Frank nodded in approval and continued to set up as best he could. He decided to try out the bed and laid down. He fit with a few inches to spare. He stretched and realized it felt good to lay down after a long drive. Feeling comfy and relaxed, he closed his eyes for a few minutes to recharge. He felt peaceful amongst the solitude. A few minutes later, he heard a thud and sat up in bed. His shaving kit was on the floor. It fell off the little table with the lamp. That's okay, he thought, time to go downstairs and hang with my friends.

He walked down the winding staircase and strolled to the kitchen where Susan was waiting for him with a hot cup of coffee. A plate of donuts was on the center of the table.

"I like the service here," Frank laughed.

The three sat around the table for a few hours talking about skiing, farming and plans for the house. Susan listened as her husband and buddy relived old times in the air force. Most of the stories were about pranks and gags they pulled on others and sometimes each other. Occasionally, a serious tone came through that reminded them that maintaining F-15s in Kuwait was a dangerous job.

The front door flung open and the kids came running into the house. They wanted to see who owned the car parked out front. They barged into the kitchen and came right up to Frank.

"Give him some space," said Bob.

"Is this the friend you said that did all the funny stuff with you in the Air Force?" asked their daughter Sherry.

Frank looked at Bob who bowed his head and chuckled. Frank turned back to Sherry.

"Yup!" he said. "The one and only."

They all laughed and Sherry demanded a story as did her younger brother Jimmy.

"There will be time for that at dinner," said Susan. "I want you two to go do your homework."

Reluctantly, the kids went upstairs. Susan began to prepare Bob's dinner to go since he had to work an overnight shift as a security guard at a research and development branch of a major corporation.

Despite wanting to start a farm, Bob had to take work as a security guard just to make ends meet. It was a few nights a week and he didn't mind. Susan's job as a nurse at the local hospital was sufficient, but they wanted extra money to finish the house.

Susan packed up dinner for her husband, who said his goodbyes. He worked from six until midnight when someone else came in to relieve him. It was a boring job because nothing ever happened which was fine with Bob because he got home around one in the morning. It was okay with him if the company wanted to pay him to doddle around and protect its research.

Susan, Frank, Sherry and Jimmy all had dinner. The kids made Frank tell them stories, hoping to hear something their dad hadn't told them.

After dinner, they moved to the living room and began talking about skiing. The kids were learning to ski. It's Maine after all. You are required to ski if you live there. Some babies are born with skis on.

As the hour grew older, Susan made the kids go to bed. It was going to be a long fun day on the mountain. A few minutes later, Frank decided to turn in. His energy was waning after the long drive and all the revelry. He wanted to be ready for the slopes.

Susan stayed up as she always did, waiting for Bob to come home on the nights that he worked. She didn't like to go to bed alone and would wait for Bob to come back. She spent her time on the couch watching television or reading.

Frank went upstairs to his tiny room and prepared for bed. He changed into his pajamas and had an odd feeling come over him. He looked around but then passed it off as being tired. He climbed into the small bed and wiggled under the covers, kicking the hospital corners out.

He closed his eyes but didn't have the same peaceful feeling of solitude he had earlier. He opened his eyes and rolled over. After a few minutes, he rolled back to his original position. Despite being tired, he couldn't get comfortable nor could he fall asleep. He tossed and turned before finally sitting up and looking around his small confines. He wasn't sure what he was looking for but felt weird.

After staring into the darkness for a minute, he realized that there was nothing there and that he was being childish. He rolled over, faced the wall with his back to the door. He convinced himself it was nothing and slowly fell into a mild slumber.

Meanwhile, Susan was downstairs on the couch. She flipped on the television and stumbled across The Maltese Falcon, a 1940s flick starring Humphrey Bogart as detective Sam Spade who gets embroiled in a search for a statue that has a secret.

It's not a scary movie but being alone late at night tends to play tricks on the mind. Every so often, Susan had a strange feeling come over her as well. It started shortly after they moved into their new home. She kept turning around, but didn't see anything. She thought one of her children may have woken up and had come downstairs, but neither had done so.

She convinced herself she was being childish and turned back to the movie, rooting for Sam Spade. She knew how the movie ended because she had seen it a few times. She loved these old movies as did Bob.

After a few minutes, she had the sensation again. She felt her heart start to beat faster. She was afraid she would turn around and see something unsettling. She imagined that somebody was at the window staring in at her, but every time she turned to look at the window, she saw darkness.

Susan decided she had had enough of this nonsense. She peeled the blanket off of her and deposited it on the end of the couch. She stood up and stared at the window for what seemed like an eternity. She garnered her courage and carefully walked over to the window.

She slowly approached, got up close to the glass and stared out into the darkness, half expecting someone to press their face against the glass from outside. She focused far and wide trying to identify someone, but it was so dark that it seemed impossible. Again, she kept telling herself that she was being silly.

Susan reached up very slowly, put her finger through the ring of the shade and drew it closed. She stepped to the next window of the turret and did the same. And finally, the third window. Her mission was complete. The shades were all drawn. Safety had been achieved.

She slowly walked back to the couch, grabbed the blanket and started to sit back down. She plopped herself down, pulled the blanket back over her legs and nestled into the corner of the couch.

She was focused on the movie for about 30 seconds when the shade on the middle window recoiled on its own, slapping against the frame and the glass. Susan nearly jumped out of her skin and ended up sitting on the arm of the couch facing the window. The blackness from the outside was exposed once again.

Susan took a few deep breaths, sunk down under the blanket until it reached her chin and focused on the movie. She was not getting up again until Bob got home. It took her a few minutes to calm down. She then looked at the dark window, put her hand up to her face and giggled. The giggle broke into a laugh and she couldn't stop laughing.

"I am so silly?" she thought.

She grabbed the blanket, sat on the couch and watched the movie again. Mary Astor was revealing that she was not Ms. Wonderly as she proclaimed, but Bridgid O'Shaugnessy and that her partner had been killed. Susan loved this part of the movie and got lost in it once again.

The feeling she experienced earlier swept over her again. The windows were drawn, except for the middle one. What could it be now? She slowly turned toward the window to see if something was there. It wasn't the window. It was the stairs. She could see it out of her peripheral. She turned toward the bottom of the stairs and saw the figure of a man.

Susan jumped and screamed again and tried to make sense of what she thought she saw. She was a breathing heavy and just scared out of her wits. Frank gently grabbed her shoulders and Susan leapt onto the couch screaming and jumping. She was seemingly inconsolable.

"It's me. It's just me. Frank," said her houseguest as he held his hands up and tried to diffuse her panic that he was partly responsible for.

Susan relaxed and looked at him wide-eyed, realizing he was the figure of a man she saw at the stairs. She processed this information but didn't laugh this time. She began to sob and Frank was unsure of what to do.

She lurched forward and gave him such a tight hug that he thought she was going to break a rib. After a minute or so, she released her grip on Frank.

"Sit down Susan," he began. "I didn't mean to frighten you. It's just that I heard you scream and came down to make sure everything was ok."

Susan looked at Frank, but didn't want to tell him she was afraid in her own house. As she searched for words, the kids came down the stairs.

"Are you okay Mommy?" they both asked in unison as they ran over to the couch.

"Mommy just had a nightmare," she said as she hugged them both. "No worries."

The kids stood there for a minute until Susan ushered them back to bed.

"You need your sleep for tomorrow."

After the kids left, Frank looked at Susan. He felt she was covering and that there was another reason the way she had acted.

"Tell me the truth," he said. "What really happened?"

Susan considered telling him the truth, but she didn't want her husband's best friend to think she was crazy. She began to speak as she searched her brain for some excuse that he would believe or at least buy for now.

"I … I saw a mouse," she said. "I drifted off to sleep and it climbed up on my blanket."

Frank eyeballed her, assessing whether that made sense to him. "And the laughing?" he asked.

"It's funny, right?" she asked. "A grown woman, a hundred times bigger than a mouse, being afraid of it. I was laughing at myself."

Frank smirked as he analyzed her comment and her facial expression. Then he bowed his head and chuckled.

"It's an old house with a mouse," he said. "It makes sense."

Susan concurred and offered a smile.

"It's late. Why don't you go upstairs to bed?" Frank asked.

"Bob will be home in another 45 minutes," she replied. "I'll wait up for him. You go back to bed."

Frank agreed and got off the couch. The two looked at each other. She wanted to tell him the truth but didn't. He knew she was hiding something but decided to let her off the hook. It was something for Bob to deal with, not him.

"Goodnight," Frank said.

Susan watched him go up the stairs. He turned back once to look at her and she offered another smile. Frank smiled back and ascended to the second floor, back to his tiny room with the tiny bed and the tiny window.

Susan breathed a sigh of relief. She wasn't sure he believed her, but she had to get over it.

She continued back to the movie. This time, Bogart was meeting with Sydney Greenstreet, the infamous Mr. G, discussing arrangements to retrieve the Maltese Falcon.

It wasn't long before the feeling returned again. Maybe it was just creepy Peter Lorre from the movie. But she knew that wasn't the case. She turned around and this time she didn't look at the one dark window with the shade up. She was looking at the bottom of the stairs.

And there was the family cat, rubbing itself at the bottom of the stairs. But it wasn't against anything solid. The cat was rubbing itself and purring like it had done so many times against her hand or leg. She could see the cat's fur folding over like grass under her feet when she walks on the lawn. She could see it happening in front of her along the length of the cat's side. And as the cat moved, she saw the fur bounce back up just like grass after you lifted your foot.

"My God," she gasped. "The cat is rubbing against the air."

Susan's eyes widened with fear as she watched their cat, Comet, rub against absolutely nothing. The cat, now satisfied with affection it received turned to her, meowed and walked away.

She stood there processing what had happened. She was trying to come up with some logical reason. The feeling had not been coming from the darkness of the window, but from the base of the stairs. Now she realized something may be in the house, standing at the bottom of the stairs, looking at her each night when she waited up for her husband.

Susan felt a queasiness in her stomach. Most of it was fear but there was amazement and curiosity as well. She wanted to ask if something was there but she didn't know what to say. And part of her was afraid she'd get an answer. She just stood there looking at the bottom of the stairs, waiting for something to happen but it never did.

The feeling finally left her after watching for a few minutes. It felt different and whatever it was had left. Now she knew why she always couldn't go to bed alone. She felt something in the house. She sensed it all along, but didn't understand her own feelings.

Bob finally came home and opened the door to find Susan sitting up on the couch with her knees up at her chest. The blanket was loosely around one side of her, covering a shoulder, leg and foot. She was wide awake as if she drank a cup of dark roast coffee after 8 pm. She looked at him and didn't move.

Bob carefully walked over thinking he had done something wrong and he was about to find out. Susan got up and hugged him tight just like she had done to Frank.

"Hey," he began, somewhat confused. "What was that about?"

"I'm just glad your home," she said. "Let's go to bed."

Bob knew that greeting was much different than all the other nights and knew there had to be a good reason. He loved Susan and Susan loved him, but that was a hug that meant something happened.

His mind raced from a problem with the kids to a problem with Frank. But Susan said nothing about what she saw, thought she saw or didn't see at all. They locked the door and shut the lights. They walked toward the stairs, but Susan stopped and retrieved her blanket, so Bob walked up the stairs first.

Bob turned in time to see Susan walk toward the stairs, hesitate for a few seconds and then quickly come up the stairs to him. He just shook his head and they walked to the bedroom and went to bed. Bob noted that Susan didn't use the blanket, but just tossed it on the bedroom chair.

The morning sun shone through the tiny square window in Frank's room onto his face. He slowly fluttered his eye lids, waking up to the smell of bacon wafting through the tiny room from the kitchen.

He tossed on his pair of fatigues and the Henley shirt that he was wearing when he arrived. He stopped at the bathroom to splash some water on his face and brush his teeth. Then he used his nose to follow the smell of the bacon.

He arrived at the kitchen and saw several smiling faces gathered around the table for breakfast. Bob made waffles, scrambled eggs and bacon. Susan made a fruit bowl. The remaining empty seat was at the head of the table.

"Good morning sleepy head," said Bob. "I was going to come and get you at 5:30 and yell in your face like sarge used to do."

Frank tossed Bob a smirk because he remembered those days all so well. Susan got up and made a plate for Frank, who poured a cup of coffee. He sat at the lone empty chair. He began to take a bite of eggs.

The kids were smiley and cheerful, but the entire revelry wasn't the same as the day before when Frank first arrived. Susan wasn't her usual self and Frank seemed slightly uneasy too. Bob wasn't sure what to make of it but realized something was up. He assumed it had to do with that hug.

"What's going on with you two?" Bob asked.

"I guess I didn't sleep that well," said Frank. "Must have been the long drive or perhaps the excitement of a day of skiing."

Susan stared at Frank and figured that maybe he had sensed what she saw, thought she saw or didn't see at all. Frank caught Susan's stare and got the impression she knew something. Bob was looking at the two of them and started having wild thoughts that something happened between his friend and his wife. Meanwhile, the kids were unaware and just chomping on their waffles.

"Is everything alright with you two?" Bob asked in a not so friendly tone.

The kids now picked up on the tension. Susan and Frank looked at each other. Susan looked at her kids and wondered if she should say something in front of them. They had to live there too and how would they take it.

"Well?" Bob continued. "What the hell is going on?"

Susan put down her knife and fork and started to sob.

"I saw something last night," she said.

"Something? Like what type of something?" Bob demanded.

"I don't know how to explain it," she said.

"It wasn't a mouse after all," Frank commented.

"Comet will get the mouse," said Jimmy. "He's got them before."

Bob stood up and looked over at Frank.

"You know about this?" he said.

"Calm down, Bob," said Susan. "Frank doesn't know anything about what I really saw."

"Then what did you see?" he asked again.

Susan took a big sigh to summon up her courage. She explained to the best of her ability that she saw the cat rubbing up against the air. Jimmy wasn't quite sure what she meant but Sherry got it and ran to her mother's side. It made sense to Frank now too. Bob sat back and was relieved for the moment that nothing had happened between his wife and friend and then began to shrug the whole story off.

"Come on!" he said. "The cat was just stretching."

Susan shook her head no and Bob continued to express disbelief.

"There was something in my room last night," claimed Frank.

"Not you too," asked Bob.

Frank shook his head yes and then Sherry piped up too about having weird feelings in her room from time to time.

"I don't feel like going skiing today," Susan said. "You all go."

Frank concurred with Susan. He was tired because he didn't sleep well. Sherry and Jimmy were now somewhat frightened by all this talk of something in the house.

"Really?" asked Bob. 'We're not going to do this? We've planned this for weeks."

They sat there quietly eating breakfast. The kids munched on the crispy waffles. Frank stirred his coffee and Susan just sat there. Bob surveyed the room and realized he had no choice.

"Okay," began Bob, conceding a day of skiing. "Let's go to the library and research the house. That's something we never did. I'll prove there is nothing to this and we'll go skiing tomorrow."

An infusion of energy filled the room and everyone concurred with the idea. They wanted to know what was going on in their home. A mystery was afoot.

They piled into the car after breakfast and headed to the library that was in the same building as town hall. After providing the librarian with their address, she smiled at them.

"You're the family that bought the old Mansfield home," she exclaimed.

They all looked at each other and wondered "Who were the Mansfields?"

The librarian brought them over to the reference section of the library where all the non-circulating books were located. There was a solitary shelf under a picture of their home that looked to be late 19th century.

"It's beautiful," exclaimed Susan. "We need to fix it up just like this."

There were a handful of books, notebooks and newspaper clippings in a folder on the shelf all referencing the Mansfields. They clearly seemed to be some of the more notable people in the town. They took them all to a table and began to flip through them, offering various facts from time to time. Susan was expecting to learn that some horrible murder had occurred in the house or it was Satan worship.

As they poured through the books, they learned the Mansfields were a family that had made a fortune as merchants in Portland, Maine. Howard Mansfield made his money in textiles and lumber, shipping them from Portland to Boston and New York. When his wife grew tired of the hustle and bustle of living in a seaport, Howard bought land and had the house built in Cumberland in 1822.

They poured through the information for a few hours. It wasn't until they started going through the newspaper clippings that Susan stumbled across the information they were looking for.

"I think I got something," she said.

Everyone stopped and looked at Susan.

"Well," Bob said. "What is it?"

Susan took a deep breath.

"The Mansfields had a live-in butler," she said. "His name was Samuel."

"The room I am staying in," began Frank, "has got to be his room. A servant would have had a small room."

Susan didn't agree or disagree, but continued.

"Funeral services for Samuel H. Pierce, who served the Mansfield family as a devoted and loyal butler for 16 years, will be held Sunday, May 6, following church services."

"What year was that?" asked Jimmy.

"The house was built in 1822 so 16 more years is … 1838," said Sherry.

"Very good, honey. That's correct. The top of the clipping reads 1838," said Susan.

"How did he die?" asked Frank.

"One day," Susan began. "Samuel was carrying a tray and tripped while going down the stairs. He rolled over several times, striking his head repeatedly, finally landing at the bottom of the stairs. He …"

Susan gasped and threw the clipping on the table.

"He what?" they all demanded.

Bob grabbed the article first and read the rest of the paragraph.

"Striking his head repeatedly, yata yata yata," Bob read. "He ... whoa! He snapped his neck and died at the bottom of the stairs."

Bob looked up from the clipping and looked at everyone.

"That means the cat was not rubbing up against the air, it was rubbing up against Samuel."

A PROMISE IS A PROMISE

G wen Norton leaned over so she could look her son Adam directly in the eyes. She put her hand on his shoulder.

"I need you to be a good boy for Nana and Papa," she said. "Do everything they say and we'll bring you back a nice surprise."

Adam nodded and his mom stood up.

"We're counting on your help, buddy," said his father David who then looked to his daughter Becky. "And you too. You're the oldest honey so you look after your brother. We love you both very, very much."

Becky nodded as well.

"Oh, the kids will be fine," said Nana. "They are always a pleasure and so easy to take care of. We love having them and are excited to have them for the whole week."

David and Gwen looked at each other. They were about to embark on a kid free, semi-vacation to London. Gwen had a conference to go to as she was a featured speaker. Then her and David were going to spend extra time in England for themselves. They loved their 8- and 10-year-old children, but every now and then, parents needed down time in the form of an island getaway. England is a giant island after all.

"You don't worry about a thing," said Nana. "We got a whole bunch of stuff planned with the young-ins."

Gwen looked at the kids and then her parents.

"Thanks mom and dad," she said. "We really appreciate you taking time out of your schedule so we could have this vacation."

"Don't be silly honey," said Papa. "We know how important the conference is and what this will do for your career. Nothing was going to prevent us from taking care of the grandkids."

After another minute of goodbyes, David and Gwen walked to

the car and drove away. The car was barely out of sight when Adam yelled, "Can we have ice cream for dinner?"

Papa and Nana let out a laugh and then came back with a unanimous "NO!"

"But nice try kiddo," said Papa. "Let's go inside and have dinner and maybe, just maybe, we'll discuss dessert."

"Ice cream?" said Adam as he smiled up at his Papa, who chuckled and ushered his grandson inside.

The four walked in the cozy Mansard Victorian house. The grandparents lived in the house for close to 50 years and loved its detailed molding, pocket doors and built-in cabinets. They adored it and the kids enjoyed coming over.

Nana went to work preparing dinner in the kitchen. Papa sat on the couch showing the kids some of their coin collection. He liked to tell them old stories associated with the coins and they would listen intently.

Nana finally called them all to dinner and they all went to the kitchen table and took seats. Nana came over with a chicken casserole and a side of green beans and mashed potatoes.

"No ice cream," sighed Adam.

"If you shape the mashed potatoes on your plate just right, you can pretend it's vanilla ice cream," joked Papa.

Everyone laughed except Adam frowned, but he knew it was a longshot anyway.

They sat there at the dining room table. Adam was picking through his plate fairly well and Becky was eating everything but the vegetables. She noticed that Papa was not eating his vegetables either.

"Do you not like vegetables Papa," she asked.

He looked at her and smiled, turning the question back on her.

"Are you not hungry Nana?" asked Adam who noticed she had barely touched her plate of food.

"I guess I picked too much while making this fabulous meal," she answered.

"We have a lot of plans this week," said Papa. "Do you want to hear what we're going to do?"

Nana put down her fork, clasped her hands together and placed her elbows on the table.

"Well," she began. "We got a few of those DVDs that you like for watching at night. But we have library passes for the zoo, the Science Museum and the aquarium. We figured we'd walk the trail around Pickett's Woods, go to the kid's park and hit the arcade too. And, we'll get ice cream one night."

The kids cheered and so did Papa. It was going to be a busy but fun week.

They cleaned up after dinner and then all sat down on the couch. Nana and Papa watched Wheel of Fortune and then Jeopardy, occasionally shouting out an answer. Adam would shout out funny answers from time to time but Becky actually got one correct when she shouted "Mississippi River" during Jeopardy.

Then they watched an animated movie that all had the usual positive spin. Adam conked out around 9 p.m. before the movie finished. Becky held off her eyelids until the Prince and Princess got married and then fell asleep.

Nana went into the kitchen to clean up. After a few minutes, a frying pan fell and made a loud noise when it struck the floor. Becky woke up immediately

"What was that?" she yelled.

"It's okay," Papa said. "Your clumsy Nana just dropped something. Time to go to bed sweetheart. Nudge your brother awake and go up the stairs to bed."

Nana and Papa followed up the stairs a few minutes later. The kids woke up enough to brush their teeth and then crawled into bed. The grandparents said goodnight and walked out the open door to their bedroom.

The next morning, Becky awoke to the smell of eggs, toast and sausage. She went and got Adam and they went downstairs to find two plates set for them, a glass of milk and a smaller glass of orange juice.

"Nana! Papa!" she called out, but she didn't see them.

Meanwhile, Adam plunked himself down and began eating. Becky followed suit. A few minutes later they heard a door shut upstairs. Adam and Becky looked up and heard the footsteps approach the stairs and come down to the first floor.

"Hi kids, how's breakfast?" asked Papa.

The kids nodded with their mouths full.

"Are you going to eat?" Becky asked.

"I already ate and so did Nana," he said. "We've been up for a while. Nana is busy upstairs, but she'll come down soon. You kids eat. I have to go outside for a few minutes."

The kids were almost done with breakfast when Nana finally came down the stairs.

"Hi kids," she said exuberantly. "Fuel up with breakfast because we got a big day ahead in the city."

The kids finished breakfast and cleaned up as told. Nana and Papa made sure the kids were dressed properly. And they started to leave.

"Adam," Papa started, "be a good sport and go get my money. I left it upstairs on my dresser."

Adam ran up the stairs and was back down quickly. He tried to hand it to Papa, who told him he went and got the money so he should hold it. Adam got very excited.

They started to walk out the door and then Nana said she forgot her purse and sent Becky in to get it. She came back and Nana told Becky to hold it because her arthritis was bothering her.

They went outside but instead of walking to the Papa-mobile, the grandparents ushered the children down the street.

"Aren't we taking your old car?" Becky asked.

"Well, the Papa-mobile is having some issues so we thought it would be best to leave it here and take the train," Papa said.

The kids cheered because they loved the train and it was only a short walk to downtown. They seldom took it and loved the idea of being able to sit backwards as the train moved forwards. It would take them into the city in about 30 minutes. The train went through a handful of other towns before reaching the big old train station.

One of the towns was Longfield that used to be a farming community. The old farmland is mostly suburban houses now but an old farmhouse from the early 1800s remains as does the debate in the town over what to do with it.

The house was visible from the train. The exterior of the home was weather worn from years of neglect. It was kind of plain looking but it had a porch in front of it. Some of the second-floor windows were broken, the chimney was falling apart and there was a dilapidated barn nearby on the three acres of land that remained of the old farm.

Adam and Becky stared at it as they went by.

"That's the old Emerson house," explained Papa. "It's been around for over 200 years. It's falling apart. Some of the Emersons still lived there when I was a kid."

The kids watched the house as it faded into the distance. Now there were new places like the old factory buildings that are now high-priced condos. The old mill site next to the river was a yacht club and shopping mall.

The train pulled into the station and the four of them walked a few blocks to the Aquarium. As they approached the entrance to pay, Adam started to take out the money.

"We don't need money for this Adam," Nana said. "Becky reach into my purse and pull out the aquarium pass that I got from the library."

Becky showed the pass at the entrance to the young woman, who scanned it and waved them through. The four of them spent several hours going through all the floors of aquarium. They finally stopped to eat and that's when Papa told Adam that he could pay for it with the cash.

A few hours later they were back on the train heading home. The kids once again could not take their eyes off the Emerson house when the train passed.

"It looks really cool," said Becky. "Can we visit it?"

"No!" exclaimed Nana. "We're not going there and you should never go there. It's falling apart. It's dangerous! You could get hurt."

Adam and Becky looked at each other. It was one of the few times that they saw their Nana get upset. They told her they would forget about the house.

But the next day when they all took the train again into the city, the kids could not help but steal glances at the old Emerson place. They couldn't help but wonder about the old house. They read enough Goosebumps books to suspect it was haunted.

They approached the entrance to the Science Museum and once again Adam reached into Nana's purse as instructed and showed the library pass. The older gentleman stopped them.

"Where are your parents?" he asked.

"We're with our grandparents," Becky said.

"Where are they? You need to be accompanied by an adult."

Becky looked around and spotted them standing over by the window that housed a display case of dinosaur plushies.

"There they are!" she shouted, waving to them. "Come on Nana and Papa."

The older gentleman looked and saw two people coming toward them.

"Alright kids," he said stamping their hand with a logo of the museum. "Go on in and have fun."

The grandparents joined them a few seconds later and they entered the museum. The kids led Nana and Papa all over the museum with exuberance. It was a fun day for them and they got to buy souvenirs. But the best was yet to come; the train ride home past the old Emerson house.

They went to the arcade the next day near the Sherman Wharf closer to home so they did not take the train. The zoo was the next day and they took the train, capturing the kids imagination about the old Emerson house once again. It was as if it was summoning them.

The next day was raining so they stayed home watching movies and snacking all day.

The following day they went for a walk in Pickett's Woods. When they were halfway through the trail, Papa took them off the trail and down a road. They came to a clearing and on the other side was Barnie's Ice Cream.

Adam's eyes lit up as did Becky's.

"It's pretty close to 5 p.m. so this could spoil dinner," said Nana, hesitating for a moment as the kids' excitement turned to sadness. "So don't tell your mom and dad you had ice cream for dinner."

The kids let out a cheer as did Papa and they trekked across the field to Barnie's. Adam got a hot fudge sundae and Becky got a banana split. The grandparents declined an ice cream, explaining to the kids that they were both lactose intolerant. Adam had no idea what that meant, but Becky knew it was a medical issue.

The next day the grandparents took the kids to the playground that was near Pickett's Woods. It was a large community complex that had a baseball and softball field, tennis courts, basketball courts, a track, skateboard park and a playground with all the latest equipment.

Adam and Becky went to the playground while Nana and Papa sat on a bench and watched. There were some other kids playing there around Becky's age and eventually they started to talk.

"Hi, I'm Jenny," said the girl.

"I'm Becky and this is my brother Adam."

Jack, Ben and Sally came over and introduced themselves too.

The kids were all playing together for quite some time and then Jenny asked Adam and Becky if they wanted to come over to her house and play on the trampoline. That idea seemed exciting to them so they ran over to their grandparents and asked if it would be okay.

The grandparents were reluctant at first but then realized they knew Jenny's parents and where they lived. It was the final stage of the housing development on the old farm. They gave their blessing and told the kids just two hours and to meet back at the playground.

They all took off and went to Jenny's house and there was the trampoline in the back yard. They took turns jumping up and down and at one point when Becky got high enough, she saw the Emerson house. She bounced a few more times and then got off the trampoline to let Jack take his turn.

"Have you ever been to the Emerson house?" Becky asked Jenny.

"I've been over a few times," Jenny said. "Do you know that it's haunted?"

Becky's eyes were as big as saucers. She was scared but curious.

"Do you want to go over there?" Jenny asked. "It's not too far."

Becky was torn because she wanted to see it but promised her grandmother. She told Adam and he wanted to go. We won't go inside, they figured they'd just look from the outside so not to get Nana upset.

Soon enough the kids were all heading over to the Emerson house. It was only a 20-minute walk down a shortcut behind some homes. They got to an old fence that marked the boundary of the Emerson house. A few no trespassing signs were visible. They slipped between an opening that only young kids could get through.

There it was in all its former splendor. Adam and Becky's curiosity was getting the best of them. The kids slowly approached the structure and eventually got up right next to it. Jenny stepped up on the porch with Jack, Ben and Sally. They motioned to Becky and Adam to join them.

They slowly ascended the stairs and stopped before the front door.

"Open it," Jack said to Jenny.

"We promised Nana we wouldn't go in," yelled Adam.

"We're not," said Becky. "We're just going to look."

Jenny reached out her hand and slowly put it over the rusted brass doorknob. She turned it and the door opened with ease. She let it go and it slowly swung open making the sounds that unoiled hinges make.

The kids all stared into the dusty old house that had seen better days. Becky peered into the room that was partially lit from the sun that shone through a window on the far side of the room. She could see some items like chairs, a table and clutter. There was a lot of dust and a few spiderwebs. A mouse scurried across the floor.

Jenny walked in first and Becky took a few steps to join her. Adam grabbed her hand, yelling no. They all stopped and looked at Adam, who was nervous.

"It's okay," Becky said. "We'll just be a minute. Nana and Papa won't know."

Jenny walked in and waved to Becky. The others followed including Adam who was looking left and right as he passed through the frame of the door.

"How do you know it's haunted?" asked Adam.

Jenny turned around and walked up to Adam.

"The last woman who owned the house was Etna Dixmont," began Jenny. "Her husband, Monroe, hanged himself in the house because their son, Hermon, was killed in the war and their other son, Troy, had runaway and was never heard from again. They say Etna died of loneliness but some say she killed herself by refusing to eat anything."

"So they are still here?" asked Adam.

"Etna is for sure," she said. "She doesn't want anyone to live here and she scares buyers away. And she won't let anyone tear the place down. She probably is not happy we're here."

Adam ran over to Becky, who assured him everything would be fine. Meanwhile, the others smirked and chuckled. They had been in the house several times before and had heard the stories. Nothing ever happened.

They walked into the kitchen and saw the old wrought iron cookstove. There were a few pots and pans and a table with a couple of chairs. There were spots on the wall where pictures had been. You could tell because they were outlined by the dust around them.

As they walked around the kitchen, the kids hear a bang upstairs. They all froze.

"What was that?" asked Becky.

"Probably a squirrel or something that got into the house," assured Jenny.

The kids shook their heads. Nothing had happened in the past and this was the first time they heard a noise. The kids walked back to the living room and stood in front of the stairs, daring each other to walk up first.

Suddenly, the poker next to the fireplace fell over and the kids turned their attention to it. A door slammed upstairs and they all looked up the stairs in horror.

"Can squirrels close doors?" asked Adam.

As they stood there looking at each other for answers to these weird occurrences, a metal bucket tumbled down the stairs and landed at their feet.

In unison they screamed and bolted out of the house and ran back to Jenny's home. They didn't stop running nor did they look back. They just went as fast as their little legs could take them, collapsing near the trampoline in the backyard.

They all laid on the ground breathing heavy trying to calm down from this terrifying experience.

"We have to go back," Becky said.

"No way!" exclaimed Adam. "No way. I'm not going back to that haunted house."

"No, not there," Becky Said. "We have to go back to Nana and Papa."

It was getting dark and it was probably later than the two hours they were allotted. But there was enough sunlight to find their way back. Adam and Becky waved goodbye to the other kids and headed off to the playground. When they got there, Nana and Papa were waiting for them. The kids knew they were in trouble.

"What did we tell you?" scolded Nana.

"We just lost track of time, Nana."

"We don't mean that," said Papa. "Why did you go to the Emerson house when we told you not to?"

Adam and Becky were stunned that Nana and Papa knew that. They didn't know how they knew. They were in more trouble now than just being late.

"That place is dangerous," said Nana. "You could have been hurt. Etna has a violent temper. She used to throw things at people when she was alive like buckets."

Becky and Adam looked at each other, remembering the bucket that came down the stairs at them. They stood there in silence looking back at Nana and Papa, who realized the kids had learned their lesson.

"Let's go home and stay in for the night," Papa said. "We'll have something to eat and watch a movie. But we're going to have to tell your parents about this."

They left the playground and got back to the house just as the streetlights came on. Nana stayed in the kitchen, heating up spaghetti and meatballs while the kids washed up. Nana and Papa didn't eat dinner because they said they just don't eat much anymore. They just sat at the table, smiled, talked and watched the kids enjoy dinner.

After dinner, it was time for another animated movie. Adam again fell asleep before it ended, but Becky forced herself to stay up until the end. They then struggled to go up to their rooms and turned in for the last night that they would stay with Nana and Papa.

The next morning, breakfast was waiting for the kids once again. This time, Nana and Papa did not come downstairs to join them. The kids watched a bit of TV but after a few hours, they figured something was wrong. Their parents would be arriving soon.

Becky walked up the stairs with Adam right behind her. She turned the corner at the top of the stairs and walked to the door of Nana and Papa's room. She knocked, but no answer. She knocked again but nothing. She finally opened the door and looked into the room to see them both still in bed.

"They're still sleeping," she said to Adam.

"They have to get up because Mom and Dad will be here soon," said Adam.

Becky opened the door wider and walked in. She went over to the side of the bed and tried to shake Nana awake but she stayed sleeping. Papa would not wake up either. But they were not sleeping. Despite their young age, Becky and Adam realized that their grandparents had both passed away in their sleep. They began to cry.

After a few minutes, the doorbell rang. Gwen and David were back. They sat on the floor in the bedroom crying as the doorbell rang again and again. Finally, Gwen used her key to open the door as the kids scampered down the stairs. They were crying as they approached their parents, who immediately knew something was horribly wrong.

The kids ran to their parents and told them Nana and Papa had died. David went upstairs while Gwen stayed with the kids. David came down a few minutes later and just stood on the stairs, making eye contact with Gwen. His countenance spoke volumes, sending Gwen into a flood of tears.

David called the police, who arrived 15 minutes later.

"It was our fault because we went to the Emerson house making Nana and Papa angry," Becky explained.

Gwen and David sat the kids on the couch not really understanding what that meant. They tried to console them and each other. The police arrived and David explained what had happened and led the cops upstairs to the bedroom. The medical examiner arrived a few minutes later.

Gwen and David asked the kids about the past week. Becky and Adam explained all of the fun they had with Nana and Papa. The zoo, science museum, aquarium, et al. It was comforting to Gwen that her kids had such a good time with her parents before they expired. It lessened the sadness a bit.

A few minutes later, the cops came down the stairs with the medical examiner. The family looked.

"Can we speak alone?" Detective Carnes asked. "It would be easier to say this privately."

He motioned his head toward the children. David and Gwen knew what that meant.

"Adam. Becky. We need to speak to the detective alone," said David.

The kids didn't want to separate from their parents again after just being reunited. Detective Cogswell stepped in.

"How would you two like to see the inside of a police car?" he asked.

The kids looked back to the parents.

"It'll be okay," Gwen told them. "We are going to be right here and you can see us from the police car."

The kids reluctantly went with Detective Cogswell, leaving Detective Carnes to talk freely.

"When did you drop the kids off with your parents?" he asked.

"It would have been one week ago from today," David responded. "We were in London."

"A week ago?"

The detective looked at the medical examiner, who shook his head no.

"You left your kids with your dead parents?"

David and Gwen were astonished at this allegation.

"My parents were not dead," she yelled as David tried to restrict her from getting too close to the detective. "The kids told us they had a wonderful week. They had dinner every night with them, went out for ice cream, watched movies, hiked and even took the train to the city a few times."

"That all seems normal so what's your point?" David demanded.

Detective Carnes took in a deep breath because what was about to be explained would not make any sense. He turned to the medical examiner for the explanation.

"In a case like this we need to evaluate TSD or Time Since Death," she explained. "If your parents had expired last night, we'd be seeing signs of the fourth stage called Livor Mortis or discoloration after death. What we are seeing up in the bedroom are signs of the advanced decomposition phase that begins four to 10 days after death."

Gwen and David stood there in shock with hundreds of thoughts racing through their mind. What does this mean? What are they saying? Are we being accused of something?

"You have to be wrong!" David exclaimed. "That would mean they were dead when we dropped our kids off. But we talked to them."

"You don't know what you are talking about," Gwen yelled. "Our kids explained all the things they did this week with them. That would mean my parents were dead and that my kids did all those trips on their own. Are you calling them liars?"

The medical examiner stood there, taking the anger from the parents. She knew it was a hard pill to swallow.

"It doesn't make sense, I know," Det. Carnes said. "But the medical examiner isn't wrong."

Detective Cogswell entered the house and showed Carnes a phone with a picture.

"That's my daughter's phone," said Gwen.

Carnes eyebrows raised to the top of his head as he stared at a picture on Becky's phone.

"You have to see this," the detective said.

He handed them the phone and David and Gwen looked at the first picture in awe.

It was a picture of the grandparents, Adam and Becky eating ice cream at Barnie's Ice Cream Emporium. The kids were in perfect focus, but Nana and Papa were slightly blurred.

"This proves that they were alive. They got ice cream," David explained. "The time since death is wrong."

"Sir," Det. Carnes began. "Barnie's Ice Cream Emporium closed about 40 years ago."

Something then hit the ground between the three of them and made a clanking sound. The detective looked up to see where it could have come from. David scoured the ground trying to find what fell. Gwen then bent over and picked up something shiny. She slowly brought it up toward her face and realized it was a shiny new 1915 Buffalo Head Nickel.

Gwen broke into a smile and then started to cry as she looked at the nickel. She knew what it meant. David stared at the nickel in amazement and gave Gwen a hug.

"Your dad was a coin collector," said David. "This is a sign from your dad."

Gwen shook her head yes as David held her. Tears streamed down her face.

"My dad said that nothing was going to stop them from taking care of the kids this week," she cried. "Nothing. Not even death. A promise is a promise."

Becky and Adam visited the haunted Emerson house for a few minutes, but the real visit to a haunted house was the one they stayed in all week.

THE WRAITH OF
TEDDY GREEN

The question of whether living creatures have a spirit was answered for me when I was 18 years old. I was not sure and only knew what the church had told me. But everyone has questions but doesn't necessarily get them answered.

I was fortunate. I had my questioned answered in the most unlikely fashion. There was no epiphany. No dead relative appeared to me. God didn't tell me. The proof came from my dog.

Let me introduce you to my dog Teddy Green. My uncle had a friend who was giving him away. He was a beagle mix about two years old when we got him. He had a lot of black hair on his back and sides. Black fur was halfway down his legs but then they were brown and his paws were white. This was all four legs.

The top of his head was black and around his eyes were black too. But there was brown fur above his eyes like eyebrows. They were bushy like those of angel second class Clarence in the movie "It's A Wonderful Life. The snout under his eyes was brown. There was a ring of white fur around his nose.

His chest was black except for the very front where a two-inch swath of white fur ran from his snout to his belly. I used to think it was like some sort of dog tie.

He had a pleasant personality but could get very excited. He had energy to spare. He was mostly docile and I have so many fond memories of him laying on my bed just chilling.

And that brings me to elaborate more on his name – Teddy Green. We didn't name him. He came to us with that name from the previous owner.

Does that name sound familiar? It should. You see, the dog

was named after Edward Joseph "Terrible Ted" Green, who played defense for the NHL's Boston Bruins. He played one game for them in the 1960-61 season and then played over 600 games for the Bruins from 1961 through 1972. He won two Stanley Cups with the Bruins in 1970 and 1972. He won four more Stanley Cups as an assistant coach with the Edmonton Oilers in 1984, 1985, 1987 and 1988 and then a fifth with the Oilers as Co-Coach in 1990.

In all, Green won the Stanley Cup seven times and had quite the storied career. But many hockey fans know him more for an incident that occurred in the early stages of the 1969 season. Green got in a hockey fight with St. Louis Blues forward Wayne Maki. The brawl escalated into a bloody stick fight. This was before players wore helmets. Green was struck in the head, suffering a fractured skull and brain damage. He missed the rest of the season and the playoffs. A metal plate was medically inserted into his head. Green died in 2019 in Edmonton, Canada.

I'm guessing that the former owner named my dog Teddy Green because he was a fan of the player. But I like to think it was because both Teddy Greens were defensemen. Or should that be defense-dog for my four-legged friend?

My dog never bit anyone or became violent, but he would growl from time to time if someone came to the door he didn't recognize. He was very defensive about his family. Hence, defense-dog.

And he was a character like I suppose the human Teddy Green was.

He would sleep in my room at night. Sometimes he would sprawl out on the rug and sometimes up on my bed. He would beat me to the bed and I would have to nudge him over. He would take it over and leave me very little room. He made himself seem like he was permanent and I couldn't move him. He would open his mouth a little bit when I did it and it always seemed like he was laughing at me.

But I would get him back by convincing him that I was making him sneeze. My dog would randomly sneeze so I would imitate him with a fake sneeze. He would look at me and then I would fake sneeze again. It caused him to sneeze and it made him think I was some sort of wizard. He would drop his head down so it hovered over the rug by a few inches. His right and left front legs would be extended in front of him.

I would fake sneeze again causing him to sneeze. He would strike the pose again and sneeze. Sometimes he would bark at me as if to say "Stop it!" I only let it repeat three to four times because I didn't want to upset him too much. I just wanted him to understand the balance of power.

Teddy Green would also jump on the couch and sleep there except for when my dad wanted the couch. He would get off immediately for my dad was the Alpha. When we weren't home, I can only imagine what the dog would do. He probably threw wild parties with all his dog friends and played poker.

I was a latch key kid so I would get home from school first before anyone else in my family. Teddy Green would run around the house wildly because he was so excited. He'd go up and down the hall a couple of times and stop on a dime on the rug as if he was doing a hockey stop. He would calm down after a few minutes and I would take him outside so he could do his business.

He was very friendly with people who came over the house. If we were calm, he was calm. He accepted anyone that we allowed in the house, but sometimes he was too friendly. He would hump their leg. He didn't do it to everyone so we're not sure what did it for him. He would walk up, grab the person's thigh with his front paws and thrust like a wild man on their calves. He did it to a few of my friends.

But the funniest incident of them all was when he got off of his chain in the backyard and went on the prowl for a lover. We had no idea how it happened, but we got a phone call. The person got our number from the dog tag which means they were able to corral my dog long enough to get the phone number.

I remember that my dad got the call and told me to check to see if the dog was outside. I went out and he was gone. I reported back to my dad and he told the people on the phone that we would be right down.

Teddy Green had gone about one mile from the house. He actually chased a female dog into the house of the people who called us. He was running around inside their home trying to have sex with their dog. And I have to admit that their dog was very cute by dog standards. My dog was in heat and was looking for love.

My dad and I entered the house but my dog gave us that "not now, I'm busy look." He ran from us and we had a heck of a time trying to get him. It wasn't until the family locked their dog in another room that my dog realized it was not going to happen. Nevertheless, he tried to bolt.

We had cornered him in their living room and he stood their looking at us like he was giving himself up. However, he was weighing his next move. He actually darted a few steps in my direction like he was going to go into the dining room. I stepped toward the dining room to block him and he made a sudden burst in between my dad and I.

That little stinker tricked me. He faked to the dining room to get me to move and open up more space between my dad and I. He wanted freedom to go find another woman and it nearly worked.

I dove back to the middle to try and grab him but my dad anticipated Teddy Green's move and beat him to the spot, grabbing his collar. We got the chain on him and my dog knew his impromptu rendezvous was over.

The family said that my dog never tried to bite them or even growled at them. He let them pet him and they did have time to look at the dog tag and get our phone number.

We got him out to the car and brought him home. Within the next week, we had him neutered. He was much calmer after that. But he still managed his typical antics. He was such a character.

One time my cousin, friend and I got steak and cheese subs at a local place and went back to my house to eat them and watch television. My cousin had a dog and was comfortable with Teddy. But my friend did not have a dog or any other pet for that matter. He was not as comfortable. And it was like my dog knew that. It was as if my dog picked out the weakest of the three humans and just keyed on him.

We took the subs out of the bags and got plates so we could sit on the couch and watch whatever it is we were going to watch. My parents owned an old Magnavox TV that swiveled. We got all the local channels via VHF and were able to pick up a few UHF channels too. Sometimes, when the weather and atmosphere were just right, we could get the bowling station from 50 miles away. If the picture started to get fuzzy, my dad would make me move the antenna. Sometimes, I had to stand there for 10-15 minutes until the program ended.

The TV had remote control, but not like the infrared devices of today. You had a little device with a 15-foot cord that you had to plug into the back of the TV. I was setting that up while my cousin and friend were in the kitchen.

I had left my sub on the counter and got a drink. My cousin did the same. My friend did not. He left his sub on the edge of the table while he went to get something to drink. My dog was lurking under the kitchen table. He could smell the food, knew my friend was the weakest link and waited for the right time to strike.

Finally, all three of us had our backs turned to the table and my dog struck. The chairs were pushed in so we figure my dog lifted himself up on his hind legs to the table surface, grabbed my friend's steak and cheese sub in his mouth and slipped back under the table. We didn't hear anything. My dog was so sly about it. At least in the movie Jaws there was music to warn you the shark was coming.

My friend turned around and said "Where's my sub?"

My cousin and I turned to look.

"I put it right here," my friend said, pointing to the corner of the table

I knew right away. I looked under the table and there was my dog between the four chrome legs of the black padded kitchen chair taking the last few chomps of a steak and cheese. And I must say he looked rather pleased about it.

"I found your sub," I said to my friend. "My dog thanks you."

My friend was not happy. My cousin and I each gave him a piece of our subs. We all had a medium steak and cheese sub except for my dog. He had a large steak and cheese sub and was very satiated.

And then there was the ghostly encounter that my dog and I experienced together.

We were all in the living room in the later hours of the evening watching a spooky movie on television. My mom was in her gold-colored cushioned club chair. My dad was stretched out on the couch. I was sitting on the floor and my dog was sitting right next to me.

Suddenly, we heard the most fantastic, stereotype of a spooky ghost howl.

"WOOOOOOOOO OOOOOOO oooooo OOOOOO oooooo OOOOOOOOOoooo," emanated from the back of the house.

We all heard it and just stopped watching the movie. We may have even stopped breathing for a few seconds.

I looked at my dog and he looked at me kind of the way Lenny Briscoe and his partner would check in with each other on Law & Order after the person of interest revealed a clue to help their case. Our eyes were wide as saucers. But my dog's ears were pointed straight up in the air like a Doberman pincher. I swear to God that I could hear my dog say "Rut Ro" just like Scooby Doo. I guess that made me Shaggy.

My mom, Teddy Green and me stayed put. But my dad, or in this case maybe we should call him Fred, got up to go to the back of the house. I snuck a peak and saw him go into my room.

Great, I thought. There's a ghost in my room. Well, we are going to have to move.

After a few moments, my dad came back and explained that the casement window above my bed was slightly opened. And the wind outside had blown in perfectly to create the ghostly howl.

Another case solved by Mystery, Incorporated and this time it wasn't old cranky Mr. Union trying to scare people off the property in some real estate development scheme.

Another living room memory was when my dog would demand

that my mother pat him. She would be sitting in her chair and I would sit next to her on the floor. She would rub my head and hair with her right hand while holding a book in her left hand and reading it.

Then she would say that's enough and I would move away from the chair. My dog would then come over and sit in the same spot, hitting the palm of her hand with the top of his head. He was trying to get her to rub his head too. I think he thought he was her other son. Sometimes she patted him on the head and other times not.

All totaled, we had Teddy for about 12 years. Counting the year or so before we got him, he lived about 91 in dog years. He was very old when the end came. He had been moving slower and one day when my mom and I were home, my dog tried to stand up and his hind legs gave way and he flopped to the floor.

My mother and I realized that we had to take him to the vet right away. It was February so we got our coats on and grabbed a blanket for the dog. He only weighed about 40 pounds at this point so I easily picked him up and carried him the car. I tucked him in and sat in the back seat with him while my mother drove.

The vet was about two miles away. We drove up a hill on a state highway and then had to take a left against downhill traffic. That short windy road brought us to the vet. I carried him in while my mom got the doors.

We didn't wait long until the doctor could see us. I carried Teddy Green into the examination room and placed him on the metal table. He sat there placidly as if he knew what was going to happen. We kind of all knew. The doctor did his examination and confirmed what we all feared. It was time for Teddy Green to leave us.

My mom and I each comforted the dog as the doctor injected the needle. Teddy Green gave us an incredible soulful look as if he was saying goodbye. And within a minute, he was gone.

We made arrangements with the vet to have him buried on the property. There was quite a bit of property behind the building and he was put in a mass grave. They did not have a pet cemetery then like they do today. There is no memorial to visit. Only a location with a number.

The drive home was somber. My mom and I did not speak in the car nor much after we got home. My dad arrived home and we told him. The three of us were heartbroken. Dinner was quiet. I went to my bedroom after dinner and just laid on my bed, wishing he was there with me cuddling up against my legs.

None of us were in a better mood the next morning. At one point my mom asked me to go out to the car to get something she had left inside. I put on my boots and opened the back door. I instinctively put my hand down to keep Teddy from sneaking out, forgetting he wasn't there.

I noticed a light snow had fallen and we had another couple of inches. I looked down as I started to step out and stopped. The four-foot square landing outside the door had paw prints over the freshly fallen snow. There were a lot of them as if a dog had come to the back door and walked in circles waiting to get in.

I looked to my left and saw one set of dog prints in the snow going through the back yard, over the fence and into the neighbor's yard. It was a distance of about 30 feet.

I looked to my right and saw one set of dog prints going about 100 feet to the fence and into the street.

I gasped as I processed what I was looking at.

"What's wrong," my mom asked.

I couldn't speak. I used my hand to motion her over to the door. My dad came to look also. They saw it and came to the same conclusion as I did.

The wraith of Teddy Green had come home one last time to say goodbye.

THE INDOCTRINATION
OF CECILIA

The soft glow of a small table lamp illuminated the room in such a way to create a peaceful ambiance. There was soft instrumental music playing that was somber and pleasing to the ears.

The color of the walls was a soft gray that added to the calmness. A strip of light yellow accented the top of the walls. A handful of decals of friendly animals adorned the bottom third of the walls.

The baby room that Cecilia had created was perfect. The crib was against the far wall with a black and white mobile above it. A small dresser for clothes, rocking chair and bassinet placed along the longer wall. She enjoyed it as an adult and hoped her recently newborn baby appreciated it as much as she did.

She stroked the tiny back of baby Robert as she recalled sitting in the rocking chair when she was near term. There was a lot of anxiety in her life in the months leading up the due date. Her grandmother was very sick and her husband Thomas got laid off. They had hefty bills to pay that came with a new home.

Cecilia worried about the development of the baby. The doctor said a prenatal test of amniotic fluid detected a potential genetic abnormality. A high-resolution ultrasound a month later did not indicate anything of the sort. The doctor said not to worry and that it was likely a false positive, but it was just another concern plaguing Cecilia's mind.

And then her mother insisted on old Italian traditions leading up to the birth, rejecting Cecilia's friends from throwing her daughter a baby shower before the child was born. It was bad luck, she argued. After the child is born, she demanded.

Her mother Erminia also gave her a Chiama Angeli that means

Call to the Angels in Italian. It's okay to give a gift to the mother-to-be before the child is born, just not a gift to the baby. It is part of the *gravidanza* superstition that has been guiding new mothers and families on traditions to follow when a new child was on the way.

A Chiama Angeli is a long pendant necklace that rests on the belly of the soon-to-be-mother. There is a small bell inside that produces a sound that serves to "call" the guardian angel to protect mother and the baby.

It is often believed that the quiet sound of the chiming bells calms the baby in the womb. It is tradition that the soon-to-be-mother wears the necklace up until the birth for protection and good energy. The Chiama Angeli her mother gave her now sits on the little dresser, wrapped around the base of the lamp, biding its time for baby number two sometime in the future.

Despite the chaos preceding the birth of her child, Thomas assured Cecilia that everything would be okay. It would all work out and they would have a wonderful family. And Thomas was correct. Their child was perfectly healthy and he got a new job two weeks after Robert was born. Everyone was happy; everything was perfect.

They were so happy that Cecilia didn't always mind the traditions her mother did. In one case, Erminia dressed the baby in the *camicia della fortuna* or a good luck shirt in the hospital while Cecilia slept.

This is a newborn-sized shirt passed down from generation to generation for each new baby in the family to wear at birth. It's usually white (or sometimes red) and made of silk or cotton. It typically ties in the back.

It had been passed down in Erminia's family for seven generations when her seventh great grandmother made it for her grandson. It was white with a stitched rose over the heart and branches of olive trees along the shoulder. Cecilia had worn it at birth so now it is Robert's turn.

When they brought the baby home, Erminia immediately put a birth ribbon on the front door with the baby's name, date of birth, weight and length. Instead of Robert, she wrote Roberto the same way she called Cecilia's husband Tomasso instead of Thomas. The ribbon also included a heart.

A birth ribbon, called a fiocco nascita in Italian, signals the arrival of the family's newest member to neighbors and community members. Most of their neighbors on the cul-de-sac in suburbia had no idea what the ribbon meant. But they figured it out when Cecilia's friends brought over all the baby gifts to her.

Erminia insisted they make *bomboniere nascita* to give to and thank their visitors for celebrating the arrival of the baby. These are small gifts like party favors that are delicately packaged sugar-coated almonds that are a traditional Italian gesture.

Thomas helped with the bomboniere nascita to please his mother-in-law and to take the burden off of Cecilia. He wasn't working at the time and didn't mind. He actually embraced some of these Italian traditions because his family didn't have anything like it. He even liked Erminia calling him Tomasso, even though he wasn't Italian.

The chaos seemed to be in the distant past but it was just a little over six months ago. Cecilia didn't have any of those worries any more. Robert filled her life with utter joy and Thomas diligently stood by her side.

She finally got up and placed Robert in the crib, covering him with a baby blanket. She watched him for another minute and spied yet another Italian tradition that her mother insisted on following.

Erminia brought in a cimaruta and placed it above Robert's bed. A cimaruta is a talisman that wards off the mal'occhio commonly known in English as the evil eye.

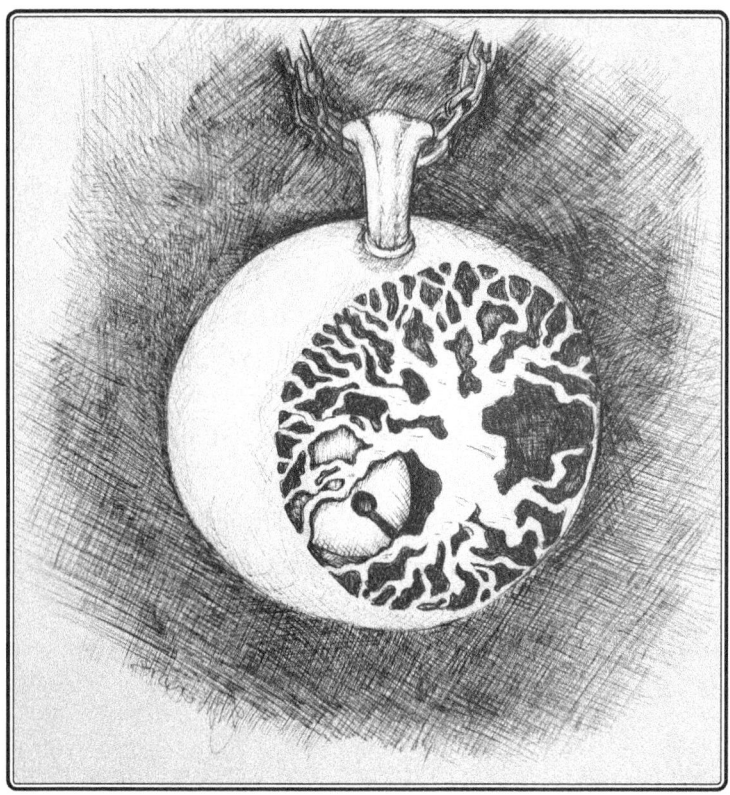

It means Sprig of Rue (stalk of the root). There are different versions designed for protection. Common symbols on the branches from the stalk are a hand, key, crescent moon, dove, rose, swords, snakes, owls, hearts, fish and more. A medieval helmet that references the great Roman General Publius Cornelius Scipio Africanus can be featured. All of these symbols are designed for protection.

The cimaruta that Erminia placed above Robert's bed was made of silver and had a hand, key, crescent moon, dove and rose that she said was the true cimaruta. It is another Italian tradition that draws from Christian symbolism.

Cecilia didn't argue with her mother about it. Robert was fine, everything worked out and everyone can use a little extra protection. Why not? she mused.

She looked back down at Robert one more time for the night,

turned on the baby monitor and quietly tip toed out of the room. She came down the stairs, walked over to the couch and plopped herself down, letting out an exhausting sigh.

Thomas came over less than a minute later with a cup of chamomile tea that Cecilia felt was the perfect end to the evening and the week.

"You seem especially tired tonight babe," he said. "Is everything ok?"

Cecilia took a sip of tea and gave him an approving smile.

"Everything is good," she began. "Everything is perfect. Thank you for the tea."

Robert smiled at her and the two enjoyed a perfect moment of satisfaction.

The sound of Robert letting out a slight cry blurted over the baby monitor to break the silence. Cecilia and Thomas thought the last few hours of the evening belonged to them, but as parents of a newborn they accepted the advice from others "not to make plans" in the first year.

"I'll go up," Thomas said. "Enjoy your tea."

Thomas walked toward the stairs as the crying turned to chuckle and a slight giggle. He turned to Cecilia and the two of them listened intently for a moment. The baby had fallen back to sleep. Robert came back to the couch.

They sat together on the couch talking and listening to music. Mostly they talked about Cecilia's mom Erminia coming over the next day. Thomas' family had just visited last month. His mother, father and sister lived clear across the country so they couldn't come as often. Erminia, however, would come over every day, if necessary.

"I just wonder what Italian tradition she's going to bring us tomorrow," said Cecilia.

"It's okay honey," said Thomas. "I like all these traditions. It's something I never grew up with so it's fine? And your mom is very helpful and supportive. It makes her feel better and so it makes me feel better that she is happy. It should make you feel happy."

"Do you believe that the Cimaruta on the wall is warding off the evil eye?" she asked.

"Well," Robert smiled. "It's harmless. Besides, there hasn't been anything evil so that mean's it's working."

"Sure," said Cecilia sarcastically. "Just like putting the couch here instead of against the wall is preventing an asteroid from hitting the Earth."

They shared a laugh and turned in for the night. They would need to get up early because Erminia would arrive early. They told her sometime after nine in the morning but she would get there before nine for sure. She only lived 10 miles away but said she never knew how bad traffic would be so it was better to be safe than sorry,

The next morning Thomas awoke to find Cecilia's half of the bed empty. He assumed she was feeding Robert. He put on sweat pants and a disheveled Henley that he had tossed on a chair two days earlier and bounded down the stairs, detecting the pleasing aroma of breakfast. He looked at the clock that glowed 9:15 in four-inch tall red LED numbers and realized Erminia had arrived well before nine in the morning as they expected. She had made breakfast, causing him to grin.

"Erminia!" he exclaimed. "Wow. This is incredible. Totally unnecessary but incredible. I could have made breakfast but thank you for doing so"

"Grazie Tomasso," Erminia began. "I like to cook. Besides you did a lot of the cooking for Cecilia and Roberto. I want to give you a break."

Thomas just smiled.

"And you took care of all of Cecilia's cravings," she continued. "Roberto does not have any birthmarks. That means all of her cravings were fulfilled."

Thomas just smiled again, accepting the compliment even though he considered the lack of a birthmark as just DNA doing its thing.

Cecilia came down the stairs with Robert in her arms. Erminia lit up like the sun sending beams of light all over the room.

"Roberto!" she exclaimed as she wiped her hands on a towel.

Erminia came over to Cecilia and took the baby to the couch.

"Ciao piccolo. Como stai?"

Hi little one. How are you?

Cecilia spoke some Italian so she knew what her mother said, but she decided she wasn't going to teach her son the language. It was just another argument between her and her mom. She looked at Thomas who just nodded his head at Cecilia to say just let it go.

Thomas took over serving breakfast as Erminia moved to the carpeted floor. She and Roberto were playing with a plushie that one of Cecilia's friends had brought over.

Thomas used their new espresso machine to make a café latte. He brought it to Erminia and placed it on the coffee table. She put the plushie down on the table to take a sip of her drink. The plushie fell off on the other side of the coffee table. Suddenly, Erminia had an outburst.

"Roberto is crawling!" she exclaimed.

The child had crawled about two feet toward the plushie that was still a few feet away. All three of them watched as he tried to crawl again, making some headway before he stopped.

"That's early, isn't it?" asked Cecilia.

Thomas looked it up on his cell phone. Babies start to crawl as early as seven months. Robert was six-and-one-half months.

"Yeah, it is," said Robert. "By a few weeks perhaps."

"Un prodigio," Erminia remarked

A prodigy.

The three marveled at the child who tried to crawl again a few times. Erminia brought the plushie closer to Robert and then just put it in front of him.

After an hour, it was obvious that Robert was tired as he started to become cranky. Cecilia took him upstairs to nurse him. And then she put him down for a nap.

Cecilia, Erminia and Thomas relaxed in the living room taking about the baby, work and current affairs while music played in the background. It was a relaxing Saturday afternoon.

The baby monitor picked up sounds of Robert stirring in his crib. A slight cry followed by a deep breath and a chuckle. This occurred a few times during a 15-minute span until it seemed Robert was awake as sounds filled the baby monitor.

"Is he giggling?" asked Erminia.

"Yes, we've heard it before mom. It's so cute."

Robert made several different sounds that emanated from the baby monitor. It was inconsistent but amusing. He wasn't crying at all but just active. The three continued to talk amongst themselves while keeping an ear tuned to the baby monitor.

And then it started.

Robert started to babble a little differently than he had been for the last two months. It was more complex with repeated sounds. Most of the sounds were hard letters like B, D and P.

They all went quiet as they focused on the baby monitor like the 1940s when people would huddle around watching the radio and listening as if they could see Milton Berle.

And then, clear as a bell, they heard what shocked their senses. It was the sound of another voice in the room with the baby that sounded like "baaaambinnno" in a soft voice.

Erminia screamed and did the sign of the cross. Cecilia and Thomas stared at each other trying to make sense of it. After letting her imagination morph into fear, Cecilia jumped off the couch and ran up the stairs to the baby's room.

There is no greater bond than that of a mother and her child. A mother carries her child inside of her and will fiercely defend that child against anything. Cecilia went up the stairs not knowing what awaited her but had the resolve of an army rooting out an invader.

She thrust open the door to see that Robert had pulled himself up to the side of the crib. He was holding onto the rail to stand but also let go of the rail and was still standing. He was shaky, but standing nevertheless.

The phrase "Un Prodigo" that her mother spoke sprang to her mind.

She noticed the curtain on the window was moving too. There was nobody in the room. It wasn't windy outside. Nothing could have caused it.

Thomas had come charging up behind Cecilia and Erminia pulled herself up the stairs much slower due to her bad knee. They also saw Robert standing in his crib. Erminia did another sign of the cross before she entered the room.

"What was that?" Cecilia asked.

"I don't know," said Thomas.

"You heard it though, right?" said Cecilia. "We all heard it. It was another voice."

"Si," said Erminia. "Delle streghe y malandanti."

"Mama please stop!" shouted Cecilia.

"What did she say?" asked Thomas.

"Witches," explained Cecilia.

"We need a priest," said Erminia. "The cimaruta is not working."

"No mama. Please stop," cried Cecilia. "You cause all this with all these traditions to keep it away. It gets into our heads and makes our imaginations see things and hear things that aren't there. It opens the door to this and evil walks through."

"I am only trying to help," Erminia explained. "The old ways need to be respected."

"Cecilia, take it easy," Thomas pleaded.

"You heard that voice Thomas; We all heard it," said Cecilia, as she took Robert and carried him downstairs.

Thomas and Erminia looked at each other for a minute not knowing what to say.

"Tomasso. You need to have a priest bless this house," said Erminia.

"No Erminia," Thomas began. "Cecilia does not believe in that and I respect her wishes."

Erminia sighed.

"But I think I am going to set up the baby camera that I bought earlier this week. I think that will put everyone at ease."

Erminia went down stairs while Thomas got the camera. It came with two rounded cameras on a base and then a monitor that could be propped up. He put the cameras in each of the two corners opposite the crib. He brought the monitor downstairs and worked on connecting it all through the household WiFi while Erminia and Cecilia talked.

"Did you mean what you said?" Erminia asked Cecilia.

Cecilia pursed her lips and turned slightly toward her mother.

"No, mama; I'm just afraid," she said. "What was that voice? What's going on.?

Erminia nodded her head.

"Did anything else happen when you went in?

Cecilia hesitated for she was afraid to say what she saw. She knew it would lead to more conversations about blessings and priests and all the sanctimony of her mother's beliefs.

"No."

"Tell me Cecilia."

"Nothing else."

"Cecilia. I know when you are holding back."

Cecilia turned toward her mother and spoke softly so Thomas couldn't hear.

"I saw the curtain moving," she whispered.

Erminia closed her eyes and opened them again all while nodding her head.

"Any other weird things happen in the house?" Erminia asked.

Cecilia turned very pensive and started to rethink occurrences in the home in the last few weeks. Some things she dismissed right away but there was another odd happening that she could not reconcile.

"Thomas was out and I was making some hard-boiled eggs," she said. "I fell asleep and woke up 30 minutes later to discover the water evaporated and the eggs popped but the gas burner was shut off."

Erminia listened intently as her daughter continued.

"I assumed Thomas came home and shut off the burner but he said he hadn't been home," she said. "I figured I may have shut it off and went back to sleep."

Erminia thought about it but said nothing to save her daughter any worries. She wanted to be certain what they might be dealing with before she came to a conclusion.

"Let me stay the night," Erminia said as she cupped her hand on the crown of Robert's head. "I will sleep in the guest room in case something else happens."

Cecilia nodded, causing Erminia to pat her on the knee as assurance that everything would be fine.

The rest of the afternoon was uneventful. Robert took another nap in the crib and nobody heard anything odd on the baby monitor. Thomas was glued to the camera monitor but didn't see anything. Cecilia stole glances here and there always looking at the curtain. She didn't see anything.

The three of them watched television and tried to pretend everything was okay but they all knew what they heard. Whatever it was, it was as if Robert knew it was there and was trying to communicate.

Unbeknownst to his wife and mother-in-law, Thomas was looking up information on the internet that could explain everything. He learned that babies generally start standing with support at seven months and the earliest they stand without support is nine months. Robert was standing with and without support as well as crawling all before seven months.

The more Thomas investigated the more he started to feel as though something out of the ordinary was happening, but he kept it all to himself.

It was finally time for dinner and Erminia had brought her sauce and meatballs. She also made a braciola that is a pounded beef filet which is stuffed with cheese, herbs, and breadcrumbs before it is pan-seared and braised in a tomato sauce

Erminia made it all the time for her husband Cesidio and daughter Cecilia. But Cecilia would not eat it. When Erminia's husband died, she didn't make it anymore. But once "Tomasso" came into the picture, Erminia made it again and Thomas gobbled it up after a few mantras of "Mangia! Mangia!" from Erminia. In many Italian households, you can get the death penalty for refusing to eat the cuisine of an Italian mother. Do not disappoint them by refusing food.

Robert was at the table in his high chair but no braciola for him.

In time, though, he would learn to enjoy it as well as his bisnonna's meatballs, sauce and homemade pasta.

Thomas cleaned up after dinner after profusely thanking Erminia for cooking. Erminia and Cecilia sat on the couch with Robert, who was exhibiting signs of tiredness again.

"Should we put him to bed?" asked Thomas.

"No," said Cecilia. "A little longer."

"He can't sleep on the couch with you or he will never sleep in his crib," said Thomas.

They all knew why Cecilia didn't want to bring Robert upstairs. But Thomas was correct. Besides, they had the camera set up and the baby monitor.

Cecilia reluctantly put Robert to bed around eight in the evening. He would wake up one more time before midnight and then hopefully sleep through the night.

They were all downstairs again half listening and watching for something strange. A few hours later they heard Robert stirring. The cry first followed by a chuckle. Then silence for a few minutes and giggling. It turned to incessant giggling.

Erminia looked at the camera monitor and saw a shadow pass in the room.

"Bedda Matri!" she cried out, causing Cecilia and Thomas to come to her side.

Oh my God

"I saw a shadow in the room," said Erminia.

"I'm sure it was just a passing car," said Thomas as he walked to the bay window at the front of the house.

The shadow appeared again and Cecilia let out a loud gasp.

"I saw it! I saw it, Mama!"

They turned to Thomas who was at the window.

"There were no cars outside just now," he explained.

Cecilia raced up the stairs once again followed by Thomas.

Erminia got up from the couch to go, but stopped and leaned closer to the camera monitor. Her eyes widened as she saw Robert standing on his own before he raised in the air a few inches and then laid down on the crib mattress. It looked as if someone picked him up and gently placed him down in the crib.

Cecilia burst through the door of the baby's room in time to see Robert slowly leaning back on the crib mattress. She looked to the curtain and it did not move. She stood there frozen processing everything in the room. Thomas came in behind her and Erminia finally made it up the stairs and into the room.

"I know who is here," Erminia said, revealing a picture of her mother in a small antique frame.

"Grandma?" Cecilia questioned. "You think it's grandma?"

"Si," said Erminia. "It is my mother, Maria Carmella."

"Okay. Alright. I want to make sure I understand," said Thomas. "You're saying your mother, Cecilia's grandmother, who died last year, is in this room right now?"

"Si," said Erminia as she walks in and places the picture on the small dresser. "It is not delle streghe or malandanti. It is my mother and the belandanti."

"And what is the belandanti?" asked Thomas.

"The protectors," said Erminia.

"I don't know if I can handle this," Thomas said.

"She died before Roberto was born but she has come to see her great grandson," said Erminia. "It's like the hard-boiled eggs. She shut off the gas burner. She is protecting the family."

Cecilia looked to her mother and realized that it was beginning to make sense. Thomas was puzzled and had no idea what Erminia meant about the hard-boiled eggs.

Cecilia stepped farther into the room, spreading her arms in a way that left her completely vulnerable. She looked around the room waiting for some sort of sign.

"Miei bisnonna," she asked. "Et tuoi?

Is that you grandmother?

There was no reply to her question but Robert giggled from his crib. And the overwhelming smell of perfume filled the room. It was a scent that Cecilia recognized all too well and Erminia did too.

Cecilia closed her eyes and breathed deeply, inhaling the pleasant odor and remembering her younger days that she spent with her grandmother getting ice cream, going bowling and going to the park.

"No doubt it is her," said Erminia as she did the sign of the cross again.

Robert then pulled himself up in his crib and went to the end of it, reaching over as if he is trying to get the picture that Erminia placed on the dresser.

Cecilia can't believe her eyes but has come full circle.

"Non andare," she begins as she reaches deep into her mind to recall the words she was taught. "Rimanere. Entra a far parte della vita di Roberto, per favore."

Don't go. Stay. Be part of Roberto's life, please.

A smell of roses suddenly filled the room. The curtain moved. It was if the room was brighter despite the darkness of the evening beyond the windows. It was a moment that the three of them shared that was scientifically unexplainable, but a spiritual certainty.

The smell of roses slowly dissipated as did the scent of perfume. Robert's giggling slowly came to a stop as he stood in his crib, let go of the rail and plopped down on his butt.

"She is gone for now, but will always be with us," said Erminia. "She will protect you and the child."

Cecilia looked at her mother with tears in her eyes before they embraced. Thomas came over and put his arms around both of them.

"Respect the old ways," Erminia whispered into her daughter's ear.

They all broke the embrace. Cecilia nodded at her mother as a tear strolled down her somber visage. She gave a knowing glance at Thomas, before she walked over to Robert. She picked him up, took the small antique frame of her grandmother from the dresser and carried the child to the chair. She looked up at her mother and smiled, before turning back at her child with an overwhelming feeling of love reserved only for first time mothers.

"Roberto," she began, dangling the picture in front of him. "Lasciami raccontarti di mia Nonna e di tua Bisnonna."

Let me tell you about my grandmother and your great grandmother

THE MATTER OF PHILIP KITTLE

It's an all too familiar situation for Philip and Cynthia.

Philip is nestled between the couch and the bookcase, standing next to the window with his arms crossed. Cynthia is facing him from the far end of the kitchen island. She is sitting on the stool with her elbows on the island and her fingers interlocked in front of her face.

They are both quiet and neither one is speaking. They have each done enough of that already. They have just had their third screaming match of the day and the umpteenth of the week. Their kids, Isabelle and Aaron, are standing near the hallway. The 6- and 8-year-old, respectively, have witnessed this latest fight. They are afraid to speak.

It seems like an eternity passes and then Cynthia puts her palms on the island and slides off the stool.

"Why don't you leave for the night?" she says to Philip. "You're scaring me and you're scaring the children."

Philip looks at her and then looks at the kids. He wonders how did they get to this point. They are fighting all the time and they have two kids. It's not ideal and it is heading in the direction of divorce.

After a moment, he briskly walks to grab his coat and heads toward the front door. He stops in front of his two kids and rubs their heads.

"It will be okay," he says before heading out the door.

Philip has no idea where he is going. A hotel, he supposes. He doesn't want to call a friend and then everyone knows.

Shit, he thinks, they all probably see the signs anyway.

He jumps into his ancient Ford Bronco. It's over 10 years old now and needed some repairs earlier this year. It rattles as he starts the engine and makes a few more new sounds he hasn't heard before. He shifts into reverse and floors it backwards out the driveway into the street without looking. He shifts back to drive and floors it again this time burning a little rubber in the process.

The house is situated on one of the largest hills of the city. He speeds around the corner and starts to descend down the hill. He is going way too fast as he comes up to the first intersection just a few hundred feet away. He sees a car coming out of the corner of his right eye. It's not going as fast as he is and he thinks he can get through the intersection first.

He realizes that was an impulsive, angry mistake and that a collision is inevitable. He jams his foot on the brakes with all his strength. He turns his head to the left, closes his eyes and braces for impact.

The high-pitched squeal of the brakes hurts his ears. He is waiting for the sound of metal crunching. It seems like an eternity as the seconds tick away. Suddenly he realizes the car came to a complete stop. He has somehow avoided the collision. He is happy but shocked.

He opens his eyes and the car that was coming passes from right to left in front of him by mere inches. He sees two women in the car, gabbing away to each other. They are oblivious to what just happened. They never stopped. They don't even yell at him. They just continue on their way through the intersection as if nothing happened.

Philip is flabbergasted that these two women didn't scream at him.

If I were them, he thinks, I would have been screaming at me for reckless driving.

He sits in the Bronco with his foot on the brake pedal in the middle of the intersection processing what just happened. His heart is racing. He is taking short breaths. He hears the honking of a car behind him and raises his hand in apology. He pulls up through the intersection and parks on the side of the road.

"What the hell just happened?" he asks aloud.

He stayed parked on the side of the road for 15 minutes until he was calm and had rationalized the entire episode. He started the engine and drove away, checking a few times to make sure nobody was speeding down the hill toward him.

Philip drove the Bronco around for a bit and finally stopped at a new place just over the town border called Umberto's. It was a pizza place and restaurant with a full bar. It was a bit out of the way so he didn't go in there often. It was perfect because he didn't want to run into anyone he knew and have to explain what he was doing alone in a bar on a Saturday night without Cynthia.

He ordered a beer and sat there, half looking at the basketball game on TV. He didn't know what to do. He didn't know how to fix this situation. The marriage counselor had given them a lot of good advice but nothing was working. He thought about his kids growing up without him and seeing them just every other weekend.

He took another swig of his beer and finished the bottle. He ordered another and when he finished that he ordered another. He was adequately addled at this point so he asked for the check, noticed the $22.50 price and tossed his credit card on the bar.

He scanned the room looking to see if there is anyone there that he knows and is happy he doesn't see anyone.

"This was declined pal," the bartender barks.

Philip gives the bartender another card and that comes back declined also. He looks at the bartender who is not pleased, thinking he is going to get stiffed.

"One second," Philip begins. "Let me see if I have cash."

He rumbles through his wallet and finds $19. One of the singles is ripped on the corner and another has drawn in eyeglasses on George Washington's face. He offers it all to the bartender, who gives Philip yet another uncomfortable stare.

"I think I have some cash in my car," he says, but the bartender provides no response except the uncomfortable stare. "I'm going to go to my car. I'll be right back."

Philip swung off the barstool and slowly walked out as the

bartender's eyes followed him out the door. The bartender knew Philip wasn't coming back before Philip knew he wasn't coming back. In fact, Philip realized he could never go to Umberto's again.

He got into his car and drove out of the parking lot, feeling the worst he has ever felt. He had another fight with Cynthia, they were probably going to get divorced, his kids were going to hate him, he couldn't pay his bar bill and his credit cards were declined so there goes the hotel for the night.

He drove around some more thinking about what to do. It was getting late so he needed some place to sleep. He figured he would do some boondocking at Walmart parking lot. He had heard that some of the stores allow truckers and campers to stay overnight in their parking lots.

Philip got there and found a nice quiet spot away from the entrance and near a lamppost. He backed in against the wall so he could see the whole parking lot. He put the seat back and relaxed. After a few deep breaths, he nodded off.

The sounds of activity in the parking lot woke him up. He looked at his phone and realized he had only been asleep for less than an hour. The store was closed and all of the cars had left except for one. He could see a guy standing next to that one car. And the guy started walking toward Philip's Bronco.

Great, he thought, as he closed his eyes and wished he had taken his gun from the house. He wasn't sure what was going to happen but the guy walking toward him didn't seem imposing so he decided to fake that he was sleeping.

There was a knock on the driver side window. He pretended not to hear it. Another knock. Another knock. Finally, the guy yelled.

"Hey buddy! You can't stay here," he yells.

Philip pretended to wake up and looked at the guy, who was wearing a name tag that read assistant manager.

"We don't allow overnight parking at this store," he explains.

Philip tried to plead with the guy to allow him to stay but he wasn't having any of it.

"No. I'll call the police," he says. "Go home!"

Philip certainly did not want the police involved because he had been drinking.

Go home, Philip thinks, there's a novel idea.

As he started the Bronco, he starts to think he should go home. It's past midnight and the kids are asleep. Cynthia is probably asleep. He can sneak in the basement door and sleep on the couch down there next to the laundry room.

He drives home and decides to park a few streets over so nobody will notice. He goes into the back of the yard and gets to the basement door. He pulls out his key, inserts it and turns the knob but it won't work. He looks at the key and it's the proper key. He tries again to no avail.

"What else can go wrong?" Philip mutters while shaking his head.

He tries another door and a few windows but everything is sealed tight. He goes to the basement door again and tries one more time. Nada. He gets the idea to try using a credit card to slip open the lock. He's never done that before but he's desperate. Amazingly it works.

"I guess that declined card is good for something," he mutters.

He makes his way to the laundry room and plops down on the couch, letting out a sigh of relief. It doesn't take him long to fall deep asleep.

Philip senses daylight through his eye lids and starts to open his eyes. He feels a hand on his shoulder and the words "Hey buddy. You can't stay here." He immediately thinks he is at the Walmart parking lot again, but this is different.

His vision unblurs and he looks up to see a police officer standing over him, shaking his shoulder.

"Come on buddy," he says. "You can't stay here."

Philip snaps awake and has no idea what's going on. He sits up on the couch and the officer takes a step back with his hand on his taser. There is a guy on the other side of the room. He's tall and balding.

"What the hell are you doing in my home?" the balding man demands

The officer raises his hand toward the man to settle him down.

"Sir, let me handle this," he says and turns to Philip. "What are you doing in his home?"

Philip is totally discombobulated. Why is there an officer there? What is this other guy talking about? They are staring at him waiting for an answer and he slowly gets his brain to communicate to his vocal cords to speak.

"His home? This is my home. What is HE doing in my home?"

"My family and I have lived here in Amesbury in this house for the last five years," the balding man yells.

"Again. Sir. Let me handle this," the officer says, turning to Philip. "You got ID?"

Just then another officer enters the room because he heard the yelling. Philip offers up his license. The officer looks at it and looks back at Philip.

"This is an expired license," he says, handing it to the other officer. "Run it."

"What the hell is going on here?" Philip asks. "I have lived here for 10 years with my wife Cynthia. I've got two kids. I don't know who this guy is over here."

"If it's your home," the officer begins. "Why didn't you use a key instead of breaking in? We saw you busted the lock."

"My key wouldn't work for some reason," he explains. "I used a credit card to jimmy open the lock."

"No," he retorts. "You hit it with something, forcing it open."

Philip kind of recalls throwing a hip into the door when the credit card trick didn't work. He realizes that he had been drinking.

The other officer enters the room and hands him Philip's license. They speak quietly off to the side. The lead officer then walks toward Philip.

"Philip Kittle. There is a warrant out on you for being a deadbeat dad. You are under arrest. Turn around."

Philip is absolutely stunned and becomes animated and argumentative. The other officer assists in handcuffing him.

"Don't make this harder than it has to be," the lead officer yells.

They read him his rights and lead him out of the house in handcuffs. As he goes out the door, he looks up to see a woman and two kids standing at the top of a landing. The kids somewhat look like his kids and the woman looks a little bit like Cynthia with her long blond hair.

The police lead Philip out to the squad car and put him in the back seat. He stares out the window to see the bald guy and the woman hug each other and their kids. He notices the house and it's unmistakably his house.

What the blazes is going on? he asks himself.

The squad car turns the corner and heads down the hill, passing through the intersection. Philip recognizes all of it and thinks everyone else is crazy. He has no idea what is going on.

They arrive at the police station and Philip is walked in to an interrogation room. He his handcuffed to the metal clasp on the middle of the table.

"Is this really necessary?" he asks, but the officers ignore him.

Philip is alone in the room for 20 minutes. He assumes he is being watched on security cameras.

They're analyzing me to see if I'm acting guilty, he thinks.

He tries to remain calm and keeps telling himself this is one big mistake. He starts to formulate step by step in his mind what happened. Two detectives finally come in. One unlocks Philip from the cuffs.

"I don't think we need that, right?" the detective asks. "You're going to cooperate, right?"

"Yeah," Philip says as he sits back in the chair.

"We just have a few questions for you?"

"Okay. Okay," Philip begins, leaning forward eager to tell his story. "Can I explain first?"

"We'll ask the questions. And I want to be sure that you know you can have a lawyer present and that this is all being recorded."

"I don't need a lawyer and you can record whatever you want," Philip answers. "This is all a huge mistake."

"Okay. Let's start then," the detective begins. "For starters, where have you been for five years?"

Puzzlement sweeps over Philip's face because he doesn't understand the question.

"Huh?" he starts. "I've been here. I was living with my wife and kids for five years."

The detectives exchange glances with each other.

"No, you haven't sir," the detective begins. "That's not your house anymore."

"Anymore? What are you talking about? I've lived there for 10 years with my wife Cynthia. We have two kids Aaron and Isabella."

"Yeah, you used to live there," explains one of the detectives. "But you bailed on your family five years ago never to be heard from again. Your wife sold the house and moved away because she couldn't afford it."

"So where have you been for five years?" asks the other detective.

Philip is incredulous and buries his face in his hands.

"What do you mean five years?" he demands. "I stormed out of the house last night and drove away. My credit cards didn't work so I couldn't get a hotel. I snuck back into the house to sleep. It's been one day. What is this five years crap?"

"Did you hit your head? Are you suffering from a concussion?" asks the detective. "Do you take drugs?"

"No … no and no," yells Philip. "They were living there as of yesterday. What are you talking about? Where is my wife? Where are my kids? Tell me where they are."

Philip stands up and the detectives stand up. An officer enters the room.

"Okay. Okay. I'm sitting back down."

One of the detectives walks out with the officer. The other detective analyzes Philip for a moment.

"My partner and I are going to talk," he says. "You sit tight."

Philip sits there in the interrogation room feeling all alone. He could be in a room with a hundred people and still feel completely alone right now. He ponders how one night can turn into five years. And then he has an epiphany. It was the near accident. Or maybe it was an accident but he survived. Something happened there.

The door opens and the detectives walk back in.

"Was there an accident at the intersection of Ridge Road and Upham Street yesterday? Or five years ago?" he asks.

"Yesterday? Not that we know of," the officer says. "We'd have to look it up, but first we are going to transfer you to the hospital for observation. We're going to have a few specialists take a look at you."

"But I'm fine," shouts Philip. "I need to know if there was an accident."

"In due time," Mr. Kittle. "First we're going to have you examined."

"But you don't understand," explains Philip before he stops

himself because he realizes they would never understand. He also realizes it would be more of a reason to keep him at the hospital. Maybe it will be an opportunity to escape.

Philip is put back in handcuffs and led out of the room to a counter in a hallway. There is an officer there who starts giving the detective in front of him paperwork. The other detective is standing behind him. He looks around and realizes there is an open manilla file folder behind the counter with his name on it. He sees a paragraph under the description heading but can't make it out. He carefully leans over the counter and can see more. This time he catches the name Cynthia. And there's an address he can't quite read. But Plaistow, NH is very clear. My wife and kids moved out of state, he realizes.

The detectives take Philip to the hospital that he has been to before. But this time they go to a wing he has never seen. It is a secure wing. A large gentleman wearing a hospital gown buzzes them inside. Philip is uncuffed and handed over to Dr. Zimmer, who walks him over to a small room with four chairs.

"Why don't you have a seat here and we are just going to talk," says Dr. Zimmer.

Philip looks at the chair tries to move it so he can face the doctor. But it's one of those detention center heavy molded chairs and it won't budge. He realizes these chairs are designed to be heavy so people who are being detained cannot pick them up and throw them. He rolls his eyes and sits, turning his body a little to face the doctor.

"Is this where I tell you all about my childhood?" Philip jokes.

The doctor smiles and writes in his notepad, analyzing that first comment by his new patient.

"We're going to jump ahead a bit Philip," he says. "Can you tell me why you think it is five years ago?"

Philip bows his head and sighs. He explains everything again in detail just like he did with the detectives. He is blowing through details because the whole time he's thinking he's got to get to Plaistow. The doctor asks a few more questions and Philip gives abrupt answers. Finally, the doctor strikes a nerve.

"Why did you ask the detectives about an accident at that intersection?" he says.

Philip freezes in his seat and stares at the doctor. He knows that if he tells him about it that he might be committed permanently instead of just a day and then how will he escape. But the longer he delays in answering, the more the doctor realizes there is something there. He is debating what to say. He knows he has to say something.

"Ahhh, it was just a curiosity," he says. "That is a bad intersection."

The doctor looks at his notepad, flips over the top page and writes some more.

"The detectives tell me there has never been an accident there," he explains. "Did you get in an accident there?"

Philip is biting his tongue because he feels there is no great answer here. He tries to turn the tables.

"What really happens when we die?" he asks the doctor, who looks at Philip very inquisitively.

"I don't think anybody knows the answer to that," he says. "That seems like an odd question to answer my question. Do you think you died in an accident at that intersection?"

Philip decides to throw caution to the wind.

"All I know is that I almost hit this other car and I don't know how I didn't," he begins. "Then none of my credit cards worked and I snuck into my house to sleep and everyone tells me it's not my house but it is five years later. I don't know how to explain it. I did not walk out on my kids and my wife. I am not a deadbeat dad. I saw my wife and kids yesterday in that house. I am not crazy. I am not a threat. All I did was find a place to sleep."

"Nobody is saying you're crazy," says the doctor in a calm tone in order to de-escalate Philip's increasingly excited tone. "You don't remember anything in between these two points in time?"

"No," he exclaims. "It's like I've jumped ahead in time by five years. Everything has changed. All I want is to go back to the night of the fight and make things right."

"Nobody can go back in time, Philip," says the doctor. "There are no time machines. Superman cannot reverse the rotation of the Earth. You exist in the time you are in. There's only going forward."

Philip latches on to that comment that there is only going forward. Maybe he can't go back, but he can go forward. He can fix it going forward. Plaistow keeps echoing in his mind.

"Perhaps you had a traumatic experience and ended up with dissociative amnesia," offers the doctor. "That's when amnesia caused by trauma or stress results in memory loss for periods of a few minutes to decades."

This is new to Philip who contemplates this idea. He was stressed when he left the house and maybe the accident was somewhere else. It sounds plausible to him but where has he been for five years. Then it strikes him that he is wearing the same clothes. What are the odds that he's wearing the same clothes five years later?

Nevertheless, he realizes that this is his way out. If he lets the doctor label this as dissociative amnesia and acts the part, the breaking and entering likely gets dismissed and the deadbeat dad label gets stripped away. It wasn't his fault. He can return to his wife and kids.

"You got me thinking doc," he says. "I just can't remember."

The doctor stands up and puts his hand on Philip's shoulder.

"You just sit here for a few minutes and I'll be right back," he says as he goes to the door.

The doctor knocks on the door and the hospital guard lets him out. Philip is alone again and now is thinking he can gain the doctor's trust and somehow use it to escape. He's got to get to Plaistow.

The doctor returns about 10 minutes later explains that they are going to run some tests. He talks about a CT and PET scan of the brain to see if there are any anomalies. He also discusses psychotherapy, medication, cognitive behavioral therapy and the remote possibility of hypnosis.

Philip concurs with the doctor and he is taken to another small room that is more like a nice jail cell. It has a bed, one of those heavy chairs, a bathroom and a window. But the window has bars on it. He looks and sees that the drop out the window is three floors down.

The doctor comes in with paperwork that Philip has to sign. He is given a hospital gown to wear instead of his clothes.

"The CT Scanner is available today at 3 pm so I booked it," the doctor explains. "We'll do that today and analyze the results. Sit tight here and we'll come get you."

Philip hatches a plan to get away. After changing into the gown, he takes his clothes and shoes over to the window that can be opened just a few inches. He slips his hand between the bars and pushes the screen off the window. Then he forces his clothes out the window to the ground below, praying they will still be there when he gets outside.

When the doctor comes to get him for the scan, they place him in a wheelchair and wheel him down several corridors. He tries to remember where his room is so he can find his clothes. He is also awaiting his moment of opportunity.

They finally get to the room where the CT Scanner is and there is another patient there. Dr. Zimmer inquires with the receptionist to learn that another doctor took the same time slot. A slight argument ensues but the result is that Philip is going to have to wait. The doctor instructs the orderly to wait with Philip while he goes to management to sort this out. The orderly then tells Philip he's got to hit the head.

Philip is alone with the other patient and the receptionist. For all they know, he is just a patient.

Is it this easy? he thinks. What is to prevent me from walking out?

"I think I am going to go to the bathroom too," he offers to the receptionist, who nods.

Philip steps out the door of the waiting room and traces his way back toward the room. Nobody bothers to question him. He finds an employee exit near where his room is located, surveys his surroundings and slips out the door. He hustles around the corner to below the window to find a landscaper discovering his clothes.

"Those are mine," he says, frantically scooping them up into his arms.

He puts the shoes on first and runs away into a nearby parking lot for another business, ducks behind a car and quickly changes. He peers out from behind the car to make sure nobody is there, puts his head down and walks away briskly.

My God, he thinks. It was that simple. What shoddy security.

Philip's plan is to get to Plaistow. He can take a bus to Salem, NH and then walk to Plaistow or hitchhike. He needs money and realizes that he is going to have to steal.

Now the police will have a real reason to put me in jail, he thinks

He considers robbing someone on the street or finding a loosely attended cash register. He looks at people walking around a strip mall and just doesn't know how to go about it. He walks into a few stores and the registers are inaccessible. They are all tablets and everyone is using some form of electronic pay through their phones. He figures maybe he'll walk away from this area and find a mom-and-pop store in a neighborhood that is old school.

After a few minutes, he spies a little convenience store called Sal's Variety. Perfect, he thinks. Probably just one person in there. He grabs a short stick on the ground for a make-believe gun and slips it in his pocket. He walks slowly toward the store breathing deeply.

Am I really going to do this? he thinks.

He waits outside the store a bit waiting until there are no customers. After some trepidation, he enters and walks toward the snacks.

Everything is normal, he thinks. I'm just a customer.

He picks up some snacks, walks to the back of the store and comes up the other aisle. He grabs a few items just to make it look good. He gets to the end of the aisle, puts his hand in his pocket onto the stick, goes up to the clerk and thrusts it forward.

"Give me all the money!" he yells in his most intimidating voice.

The clerk steps back with his hands up.

"Give me all the money now Sal!"

The old man opens the register, putting the money on the counter. He does it so quickly he drops a few. He makes Philip believe that he is nervous and bends over to pick up the fallen 20s. Instead of coming up with the 20s, he comes up with a gun.

Oh, shit! Phillip thinks. You don't bring a stick to a gun fight.

Philip pulls his hand out of his pocket to put it up in the air. The old man thinks Philip is pulling out the gun and takes aim at him. Philip realizes he's going to be shot at so he runs toward the door without hesitation just as Sal fires. Philip hears the pop of the striker hitting the primer. He senses a few bullets whizz by him. He gets out the door and runs back toward the strip mall. He stops and checks his body to see if he was shot. Nothing. He got out alive. He starts running again.

He stops at the end of the mall where he saw a vacancy before. He figures there are less people down that end and he can catch his breath. Much to his surprise it is a coffee shop and it is busy. He tries to figure out how he didn't notice that before.

He's finally breathing normal and walks out to the front of the cafe. A man comes out from the cafe and recognizes him.

"Philip?" the man shouts as he's holding a tray of three coffees. "Philip Kittle"

Philip turns around thinking it was a detective, but it is not. It takes him a second or two to realize it is Richie Warner from high school. He is amazed to see him and realizes this is the first person to recognize him from his past.

"How the hell are you?" says Philip as he walks toward Richie. The two do a bro hug.

"Great to see you buddy," says Richie. "How long has it been?"

"Time," says Philip. "What is time?"

"Are you going to the 40th high school reunion this Saturday?" asks Richie.

Philip pauses and does some quick math in his head.

Oh no, he thinks. Did it happen again?

"Wouldn't miss it," says Philip, who is still trying to figure out the latest chapter in this sordid ordeal.

"You know, I heard Cheryl McCarthy is going," winks Richie. "I had a crush on her and I know you did too. Hell, we all did. She is hot and available I understand."

"Looking forward to it," says Philip.

"Hey, I gotta meeting to go to buddy," says Richie. "Great seeing you. We'll catch up at the reunion. Go Woodchucks!"

Richie walks away after imitating a Woodchuck and Philip starts working things out. He's met a friend so he figures he's back from whatever nightmare that was before. But how. And then he realizes the incident at variety store. He didn't make it. Sal shot him. Sal killed him. He has returned to another version of his life. Death is a catalyst. It is the end of one life and the beginning of another.

He starts to think about the 40th reunion. He knows he is 58 years old now. He walks toward the glass window of the café and looks at his reflection. He's got a few wrinkles and he can see specks of gray in his hair.

My God I look like my dad, he thinks.

The other realization Philip comes to is that still probably lives at the house he "broke into." He is no longer a deadbeat dad. That Philip is dead. The Philip who got in the accident is dead. He is another Philip, who still lives on the big hill with his family.

The kids are, oh my God, they're 24 and 26, he postulates. I missed their childhood.

Despite his being older, he is still very excited that they are together as a family and he has to get there. It is only a few miles of a walk. He can be home for dinner. He starts off with a quick gait and is practically running. He has a silly smile on his face. Nothing else matters to him. He is laser focused. He is going home.

But in his zeal to get home, Philip doesn't realize the light has changed and he walks across the main road against the light. He gets halfway across when a truck comes speeding at him. He turns to look at it and has no chance to get out of the way.

"Oh shit! Not again."

Philip is on the sidewalk waking up from his latest death. He was thrown about 60 feet from the road. He seems fine. No broken bones. No blood. Not a scratch.

"You have to watch where you are going old man!" yelled a young woman in a mini-cooper. "I almost hit you!"

Philip realizes it has happened again. Now he's an old man. How old? he wonders. Does he still live on the hill? Does he still have his family. He has to go home and find out.

He looks around trying to figure out which way to walk. It's only a few minutes when a car slows down going past him and beeps the horn. He looks and hurries his pace because he has no idea what is going to happen now.

The car does a U turn in the street, drives past him and turns into a small parking lot ahead of him. Philip stops in his tracks. A young man gets out from the driver's side of the car and stands there.

"Dad!" yells the man, who is walking toward him. "Dad. It's me Aaron."

Philip looks at the man who says he is his son. It looks like Aaron but he is not 24. He's older. Mid 30s perhaps. He is happy that he is recognized again even if he doesn't recognize his son. He is also overjoyed to see his son, but he's all grown up and he missed half his life.

'You can't just walk out like that," says Aaron.

"I was going to the store," says Philip.

"You don't need to go to the store dad," Aaron sighs. "We do all that for you. I'm taking you home. Everyone is waiting for you."

"Everyone? Who's everyone?"

"Everyone dad. Mom. Isabella, my wife Emily and our daughter Phoebe."

Philip smiles and starts to cry. He can't believe his ears. He's home and has his family and a daughter in law and a granddaughter.

"You're married?" asks Philip. "How old are you?"

Aaron looks at his dad and tears up a bit. He hates seeing his dad like this. All those years of providing for the family and working in a highly technical job and now his memories are all distorted.

"Yes dad, "he says calmy. "Emily. Remember? And I'm 38."

"Oh, right. Emily," says Philip who calculates that he is now 70 years old.

"And your daughter is how old?" asks Philip.

Aaron swallows hard because he has answered this question many times before.

"Phoebe is 3 years old today. Everyone is at the house for her birthday party."

Philip looks straight ahead and tears well up in his eyes. This is all too much.

Aaron's cell phone rings and it is his mom.

"Yeah, I found him," he begins. "We're coming home. We'll be there in a few minutes."

Philip cannot distinguish all the words being spoken to Aaron, but hears his son's response.

"We can discuss what to do about his Alzheimer's later," says Aaron. "Let's just enjoy the party today."

Aaron turns to his dad and offers the phone.

"Do you want to talk to Mom?"

Philip flashes a smile that speaks volumes. What was yesterday was now years ago. He has missed a lifetime. He doesn't understand but he doesn't care. He is going home. He reaches out, takes the phone to his ear and smiles.

"Hello Cynthia," he says as his voice cracks from the overwhelming emotion coursing through his body. "I'm coming home."

Mansion on the Ridge

The storyteller gathered his guests in the middle of a room on the second floor of the Mansion on the Ridge.

"I have a bit of a spooky story to tell you," he said as the small group stopped chatting and turned their full attention to him. "It is not "make you jump scary" and not gory, but it will just make you rethink all the creaks, groans and all the other sounds that an old mansion like this makes."

"I love stories like this," said one of the women.

"Okay," said the storyteller. "Are you all ready?"

Every one of his guests nodded their head with approval. He smiled at them, waited a few seconds and then began to tell the tale that he told twice, thrice, quadrice and more.

The winter of 1995-96 was a particularly snowy one in the greater Boston region, he explained. Over 107 inches fell in the area that year, setting the all-time record that would be eclipsed about 20 years later. The metropolitan newspaper cleverly had a picture of a Boston Celtics player on the front page, measuring the snow by how high it would be on him. It was first up to his knees, then waist, chest, chin and eyebrows until it finally buried him.

Despite the massive amounts of snow, Constance had a job to do and was determined to get it done even if letter carriers had foregone their credo of "through sleet and snow, blah, blah blah" that winter.

Constance worked here at the historic Mansion on the Ridge. She had some work to do that February day for a grant that was due by mid-month. It was not snowing when she arrived at work that morning but the weather abruptly changed and had ravaged into a blizzard. Her son's school cancelled the second half of the day so she had to leave to go get him.

The school was not that far and the winding road that traversed the hillside wasn't that bad at all. She gathered her eight-year-old son Jeremy from the school and was planning to just go home and work on the grant the next day. But guilt and a looming deadline made her reconsider.

"Okay kiddo," she said as she slid into the driver's seat, closed the door and turned to look at her son. "Mommy has got to finish some important work today so we're going back to the mansion. It will be less than an hour. What say you?"

Jeremy let out a cheer as he lifted himself against the restraint of the seatbelt. Constance turned back, started the engine and took a deep breath.

"I love the mansion," said Jeremy. "Can we sleep over?"

Constance shrugged and thought the storm may force them to sleep over. That was not her plan but Mother Nature has a way of changing your plans. Yet, she appreciated the zeal her son had for the old mansion for she had it too. The apple didn't fall far from the tree which was the appropriate phrase because of the apple grove near the historic place.

The Mansion on the Ridge had been there since the late 1680s. It was originally a smaller farm house built by a family accused of witchcraft during the 1692 Salem Witchcraft Trials. None of them were executed, but they moved away after the hysteria to Western Massachusetts. Another family bought it, added to the house and stayed for a few years.

Several families since had owned the house staying for a decade or less. There were many deaths in the mansion throughout the centuries including children. Eventually, the mansion fell into grave disrepair in the mid-20th century when the city acquired it to save it from demolition.

It was appropriately named the Mansion on the Ridge because so many families had lived there it was hard to name it after just one family. Now it was a historic landmark and a favorite tourist attraction nearly year-round, except for the brutal winters when traveling the winding road could be risky.

As Constance slowly maneuvered toward the mansion, she started to rethink her decision. But she was more than halfway there and, well, living on a prayer that her decade old metallic Accord could make the trip with just front wheel drive.

She breathed a sigh of relief as she got to the gravel driveway.

"Okay kiddo," she said. "What say you?"

Jeremy answered with his actions by opening the door and jumping out of the car. Constance just smiled as she got out of the car and followed her son to the front door.

"Tell me again about grandpa and those words," Jeremy demanded.

Constance laughed as she opened the old wooden door with a latch that had been repaired multiple times over the years.

"Well, your grandpa, my dad, was a lawyer and then a judge," she said as she closed the door behind them. "When he was a judge, he would ask that question of the jury foreperson who would then read the verdict. He said that phrase to me and mom all the time so I say it to you. It's tradition."

Jeremy smiled and walked deeper into the house saying the phrase a few times. She watched him and admired the thick wooden beams that supported the frame. The plaster that covered the walls was a mixture of clay, lime and horsehair that had stood the test of time. The floorboards were very wide which was common for the day. There was a slight musty odor in the place that took a little getting used to.

Constance placed their coats on a bench in a little side room. She tracked down her son in the everyday room of the house as he said the "What Say You?" phrase once again.

She gave him instructions for the short time they would be there.

"No running. No touching. Do not pick anything up. Look with your eyes; not your hands. Hands in your pockets. Do not go in the attic," she rattled off to him. "What say you?"

"Yes mommy," he said.

Constance watched her son for a moment as Jeremy went toward the fireplace at the end of the everyday room. Then she slipped away to the office in the opposite corner, sinking into her chair to finish editing the need statement and objectives for the grant. She figured she'd save the budget for another day after the storm.

Her office was a tiny space tucked away in the corner of the mansion. It was not like the historical society could afford anything elaborate. The office was next to the ancient kitchen so the historians thought it might be a storage area for grains, flour or other cooking needs at the time.

The desk was merely a writing desk with a middle drawer that wouldn't slide open all the way. It nearly reached from one wall to the other so she had to scoot between the remaining few inches between the wall and the desk to get to the chair. She called it the crab walk because she was walking sideways like a crab.

There was a two-drawer file cabinet under the desk on the left side and a plastic rolling drawer unit underneath the right side. There wasn't enough room to put her legs between the file cabinet and the rolling drawer unit so she had to roll the drawer unit against the wall.

Anytime she got up to walk out of the office, she had to roll the drawer unit back under the desk and then do the crab walk through the eight-inch space. It was a real pain in the butt when they were open during tourist season, but she didn't mind. At least, that's what she told herself.

She knew this was what she signed up for. History was her passion which is why she spent eight years of her life going to school. First it was Williams College in Western Massachusetts for her Bachelors and then Harvard for her PhD. She had considered teaching, but she liked the research, curator and archivist parts of her occupation. She gave lectures from time to time, but she wanted to be on-site and in the trenches.

Constance also considered law school so she could follow in the footsteps of her dad, who always told her that she had a great aptitude for the law. While a career in law was tantalizing, she eventually decided on the pursuit of history.

Her father then focused on his grandson, gently nudging him toward the law with various stories about his successes. After all, the Pikes had a long history of fairness and righteousness going back to the Salem Witchcraft trials when their ancestor argued against the prosecutions and hangings.

Being the manager of the Mansion on the Ridge and sitting as a board member of the historical society and the local museum was something that fit her goals. It's just that she thought she'd have a nicer desk.

Constance got absorbed in her work but could still hear her son's footsteps in the mansion. He was still saying the "What say you?" phrase from time to time too, which made her chuckle. She was watching the time because she didn't want to stay that late and get stuck there despite her son's wishes to stay over at the nearly 350-year-old structure. He was upstairs now looking around in the master chamber.

She delved deeper into her work and got into a good flow. It was coming along well and she felt very good about the progress. She skimmed over it one more time. She dotted her "I"s and crossed her "T"s. Another skim over it perhaps. She liked what she had done but wasn't completely satisfied. They needed this grant and this had to be her best pitch yet. She had more work to do on it.

Constance sighed then listened for her son but she couldn't hear him walking around. She listened intently for the sound of something upstairs, but heard nothing. The mansion was old so sound traveled throughout the structure easily. She should be able to identify which room he is in.

Her spidey-sense kicked in. All moms have that. They know that when it is too quiet, the kids are up to something. She decided it was time to track him down and see what was going on.

Constance stood up, slid the drawer unit over and did the crab walk to get out of the office. She walked into the kitchen that was next to the office. He wasn't there and there was no evidence that he had ever been in the kitchen.

The next place she went was the everyday room. That was the room where the family gathered. It was the largest room in the home, but he wasn't sitting by the unlit fireplace or the window that were two of his favorite spots.

She made her way up the narrow and steep stairs to the second floor, making sure to hold the handrail that was added. The first room on the right is the children's room. She briskly walked into the room to only find some antique toys on an old bookcase that was in a glass display case. There were children's shoes in a display case on the other side of the room. Easels with signs on them explaining the objects stood in the corners. Jeremy was not there.

Constance walked out of the room to the master chamber and called her son's name as she crossed the threshold. But he was not there. All she saw was the usual items. There was a small antique bed frame and a table that had a wooden bowl that looked like some sort of early wash bin. Both were cordoned off by a string that passed through a few museum quality stanchions.

This was upsetting to her because she had just looked in all the rooms he should have been. And then her countenance turned grim as she realized that he must have gone up to the attic. The attic was where the servants stayed in the old days, but the wooden floor boards were a bit in disrepair. It was used for light storage. They did not allow anyone up there except employees.

She peeled off to the stairs that led to the third floor. She unclipped the plastic white chain that had an "Employees only" sign hung on it.

"Jeremy!" she yelled as she carefully ascended three steps. "You come down here right now."

She ascended a few more steps and yelled again.

"Jeremy! What say you?"

She went up the remaining steps to the room. She did a 360-degree slow turn and saw nothing out of place to indicate that he ever came up to the attic. Nevertheless, she carefully walked around the room looking behind boxes, opening a rickety closet door and looking in an old chest. She even got down to one knee at the fireplace, sticking her head in to get a look up the chimney.

It was at this point that she completely freaked out. She had checked the whole mansion. She needed to look in fireplaces, chimneys, closets and under beds in the other rooms on the way down.

Constance raced down the stairs and went to the master chamber but her second search did not produce him. The children's room was empty too. She thought that maybe he went downstairs when she went to the attic so she navigated the narrow and steep stairs as quickly as she could.

Nothing. He wasn't anywhere. Panic gripped her because her son had seemingly disappeared. It was totally unlike him.

She decided to check outside, thinking that he stepped outside the door and it locked him out. She dashed to the front door and pulled it open to see that the storm had gotten worse and now they needed to go or they would be sleeping over.

And just as she was about to step outside, she heard him. He was upstairs. It was coming from the children's room. She wondered how she could have missed him.

Constance closed the front door and ventured up the stairs again. She could hear him talking. She got to the top of the stairs, toward the children's room and stopped dead in her tracks. Jeremy was standing in the middle of the room. He was talking to the wall. There was nobody there.

Jeremy did not notice his mother standing in the doorway. She watched him in confusion as he talked and stopped as if he were listening to someone else talk. Finally, he turned his head toward his mother.

"Hi mom," he said.

"Hi honey," she replied. "What are you doing?"

"I'm talking to the boy," Jeremy said as he pointed at the wall.

Constance did not see anyone.

Jeremy turned back to the wall and then quickly turned around to face his mother.

"He's gone," he said. "You scared him away."

It was at this point Constance started to tremble. She had no idea what was happening. She considered the possibility that her son was having some sort of episode. She didn't know what to do. She didn't know what to say. She was having a panic attack on the inside and didn't want her son to know. She finally fought through the anxiety of the situation and spoke.

"Mommy's done with her work; It's time to go," she said.

But Constance was not done with her work. She wasn't even close. She wanted her son out of there as well as herself.

They hurriedly walked down the stairs and grabbed their coats. Constance did not even go to the office to fetch her computer and all the paperwork. She left it as is and the two of them got in the car, drove down the winding road and went home.

A few weeks after the grant proposal was completed and submitted, Constance quit as the manager of the Mansion on the Ridge. She never gave a reason. She just quit. But we know why.

There was silence in the room as the story teller stood in the middle of the children's room after he finished telling the story to a small group of guests inside the Mansion on the Ridge.

"Whatever happened to the little boy?" asked one of them.

The story teller looked at them for a few seconds.

"Constance's son?" questioned the story teller. "He has no recollection of the incident. He has never been back here nor has his mother. He did become a lawyer and works as an assistant district attorney for the county."

"And the mother?" another one asked.

"I heard she is working as a professor at a nearby university," the storyteller said.

Many of the people in the group had heard the story before but loved hearing it again. There were some that had never heard it. They cheered. The sound of the front door opening could be heard.

"Oh, we're going to have to disappear for a little bit," said the storyteller. "We can't let the living see us or they will freak out."

"Wait! Wait!" said another. "What happened to the other little boy that the mother's son was talking to?"

The storyteller paused and slowly broke into an ear-to-ear grin.

"I am that little boy," he said.

THE MYSTERIOUS NEIGHBOR

The overcast day matched the mood of the day. It was one of those off and on light rainy days where you would rather be home binge watching the latest hit drama on a streaming service than standing outside at a funeral.

Perry was glad to finally get home to his second-floor apartment in a neighborhood of Greater Boston. He didn't even go to the gathering after the funeral because he couldn't bear it any longer.

He lived in a triple decker which was three apartments stacked on top of each other. Often known as Irish battleships, they lined the streets of many greater Boston neighborhoods. The units would be occupied by strangers but they could also be occupied by entire families.

Perry walked in, grabbed a beer from the fridge and sat on the couch. This funeral was the toughest one he had attended. This was his third funeral in his young adult life. One was his aunt and another was an uncle. He didn't count the funerals of his grandfather and grandmother because he was young and doesn't remember much.

This funeral was for the woman who lived above him on the third floor. Chloe moved in about a year ago and they hit it off. He helped her move in and she reciprocated by making dinner for him. One thing led to another and they slept together. They had become a thing and the relationship was going into unchartered territory for him. He wasn't sure how he felt and where he wanted this to go. He was 30 years old now and maybe she was the one.

But fate reared its ugly head. One day, Chloe collapsed at work, was rushed to the hospital and died. They said it was sudden cardiac death from an undiagnosed heart problem. She was only 28 and he was stunned. His feelings were all churned up and he sat there staring at the wall. He never experienced loss like this. He had never known anyone that young who had died. It was ripping him apart.

He spent the rest of the day in a morose state, just puttering around the apartment. He would have to go to work the next day so he needed to deal with this as best he could because morning would be here before he knew it.

Perry got through the rest of the week, working his middle management job at the headquarters of a supermarket chain. He was glad that Friday finally arrived and he was looking forward to the weekend when he could just fall apart.

He didn't even go out Friday evening with his friends; instead, he went home, ate a little something, guzzled a few beers and just crashed on the couch. He awoke the next morning to sounds of banging on the third floor. It was not even 8 am and he was annoyed. Chloe's family had moved everything out during the week so he wondered what the hell the landlord was doing.

Perry got up and marched upstairs only to learn that it wasn't the landlord but a new tenant. He was surprised that someone was moving in this quickly and was upset by it. And then he met the new tenant.

"Hi, I'm Samantha," she said as she held out her hand. "I'm your new neighbor. Sorry for the early move in. It was the only time I could get the movers."

He realized this was very similar to how he had met Chloe, but stars were not in his eyes this time. He kept thinking of Chloe.

"It's ok," he mustered as he shook her hand. "Welcome to the triple deckah."

Samantha didn't offer any information about herself and he didn't ask. The two movers came out of the apartment and almost knocked him over. He looked at their faces and they were all business. It was her characteristic also.

"I'll get out of your way because you have work to do," said Perry as he excused himself.

Samantha simply smiled as she watched him go down the stairs.

Perry tended to keep to himself and didn't interact with Samantha much. He seldom saw her too. It was similar to Jill, the woman on the first floor. She didn't interact with Chloe at all and didn't attend the funeral. Now the building was full of ships just passing in the night.

Perhaps it was better this way, he thought, so Perry focused on work, staying later so he spent less time at home. He started to go out with friends but was still somewhat withdrawn. And then the stress of everything began to transmogrify into bizarre dreams.

The first strange dream he had he was walking down a road in a neighborhood he didn't recognize. The houses were bright and colorful. He had no idea where he was. He saw nobody in the dream and then arrived at a cliff that overlooked the ocean.

That's when he woke up. He remembered the dream vividly. The distinct lavenders, pinks and yellows of the homes. The sharp blue of the ocean and the green of the palm trees.

"An Island," he thought. "I was at an island."

Perry chalked up the dream to stress and that his brain was telling him that he needed a vacation. He thought it would be wonderful to get away but he couldn't afford that so he put it out of his mind.

A few days passed and he experienced another dream. It was the same dream except this time he jumped off the cliff, causing him to wake up in a sweat. It was about three in the morning and his heart was racing as he sat up recalling the dream.

A few seconds later, he heard Samantha upstairs get out of bed and walk around her apartment. He figured he woke her up and felt bad, but a sinister thought of "now we're even" crept into his head.

Perry eventually got back to sleep but he remembered this dream for weeks. He tried to figure out what it meant. He went from thinking it was a sign to take a vacation to him contemplating suicide by jumping off a cliff. He convinced himself it wasn't suicide. He felt the saddest he had ever felt in his life, but he surely did not want to end it all.

He tried to put it out of his mind as he went about his life. Weeks went by and everything seemed normal. And then the dream returned again, causing him to spring awake in the early morning with an audible yell.

This time, he recalls people following him which is why he jumped off the cliff. He also remembers the phone number 217-287-997 something. He grabbed his phone and entered the number. He was going to call each of the 10 possible numbers, but hesitated before pushing the button on the first one. Instead, he searched the area code of 217 and learned it was Illinois.

"Why do I have an Illinois phone number in my head?" he asked himself.

He then hears Samantha walking around upstairs. He thinks he woke her up again and now he feels bad.

Perry lays in bed wide awake just trying to understand what it all means. It takes over an hour for him to fall back asleep. In the morning, he heads down the stairs to go to work and is greeted by Samantha coming up the stairs.

"Hello," he said as she walked by. "I'm sorry if I woke you up last night. I have been having nightmares."

"I don't think I noticed," she said, carrying a bag of groceries. "I'm a deep sleeper."

"I heard you walk around after I woke up."

"Oh really? I maybe went to the bathroom. I don't recall."

He was a little surprised she didn't realize he yelled in his dream.

"I've got to run," she said bolting up the stairs. "I have a remote meeting for work in a few minutes."

Perry went to work and didn't worry that he woke her up. He did think of it now and then and he wondered how often she and him were up at the same time in the middle of the night. She was pretty quiet and worked from home most of the time. Her car was always in the driveway when he left for work. There were occasional times when he came home and she was out.

He decided he was going to try to focus on how many times he woke up in the middle of the night and heard her up. Maybe she was waking him up, he mused. Over the next few weeks, he kept a mental record and it occurred three times. All in all, it was about a half dozen times that they were both creatures of the night.

The more he kept track, the more he realized it was a lot more common than he thought. He started to believe that maybe something in the house was keeping him up. His mind turned to Chloe. Was her spirit waking them both? Is that possible.

The week was almost over and Perry got a text message from David about going to the pub that night for some beers, grub and girls.

Black Spectral Pig 2nite at 7

IDK

Come on!

Tired

Danielle is coming

IDC

RU OK?

No

UR crazy

Next time

Perry put down the phone and finished a report he was working on. He grabbed a small pepperoni pizza on the way home and went to his apartment. He grabbed a plate and a few napkins. He sat down at the kitchen table, opened the box and carefully picked a piece that had a giant bubble on the well-done crust. He loved those half burnt crust bubbles. He raised it to his mouth but there was a knock at the door before he could even take a bite.

"What the F***?" he said, rolling his eyes.

He opened the door only to find David standing on the other side.

"You're crazy if you think I am letting you miss this opportunity buddy," he said as he burst through the door.

"Come on in," said Perry. "Make yourself at home."

"Yeah. I will," he said grabbing the slice that Perry had grabbed for himself. "What's wrong with you?"

"Really?" Perry asked. "You can't figure that out!"

"This is different man," he said. "What's going on? Talk to me. We've known each other since 6th grade."

Perry finally shut the door and stood against it with his arms crossed. He looked at David and realized that maybe it was time to tell someone.

"Sit," said David. "Talk to me, bro."

Perry grabbed a chair and plopped himself down. David gave him a slice of pizza but it just sat in the plate. After a moment of thinking how to start, Perry opened up and told him about the sleepless nights, the weird dreams and the coincidences with Samantha upstairs.

"That's it?" David began. "Trouble sleeping. Go get a prescription for sleeping pills."

"It's more than that," Perry argued.

"What? The woman upstairs," David said. "Look, you were sleeping with Chloe and she's out of your life. I get it. It sucks. It will take time to move on, so I get not being ready to move on Danielle."

"It's affecting everything in my life," said Perry.

"Maybe you need to talk to someone. Professionally," he said. "I'll talk with you all you want, but you might need someone with better skill sets than me who can help you work this out."

"A psychiatrist?" said Perry.

"Hey, don't think of it that way. I went to one when I was having trouble with my parents' divorce. He really helped me. You never get over it, you learn to live with it."

Perry grimaced in a way that said he didn't want to go down that road.

"You never saw a psychiatrist when your dad died," David

continued. "You should have seen someone then and you definitely need to see someone now. You can't bottle up your feelings man. It will tear you apart and lead to depression."

Perry looked at David and gave it deeper thought. He knew his friend was right and appreciated the concern. Before he could speak, David pushed the issue.

"I'll get you his number," David said. "For now, eat up. We're going out, but not to the pub. We'll go somewhere else. I don't want you to be alone."

The pair had quite a night, starting off with a few drinks at a couple of dives, before heading to the nearby casino. It was a guy's night out and it ended at a trendy bar with bowling and ax throwing. Perry wondered if ax throwing was appropriate in his state but David insisted and the two had a glorious time.

The next morning Perry woke up with a slight hangover. It was just almost 11 in the morning. He checked his phone to find that David had texted him the number of the psychiatrist. Perry put the phone down and struggled out of bed. He puttered around the apartment in his sweat pants, made something to eat and turned on the TV.

After a few minutes, he grabbed his computer and searched the doctor that David had sent him. His name was Dr. Alfred Lynch. He was well known in his area of treating emotional disorders. He noticed that hypnosis was one of his treatments that was not considered mainstream.

He scrolled down and saw some other information about Dr. Lynch. He had won an award, was recognized for service and was featured in a psychiatry magazine. He checked the second page and saw more of the same until one article caught his eye. Dr. Lynch had treated a patient who believed they were abducted by aliens.

"You're not probing me pal," he said aloud and shut the computer screen.

Perry spent the whole day in the apartment. He could hear Samantha upstairs from time to time. He was wondering how she could stand being in the apartment day after day. He decided to sit on his deck and enjoy the decent weather. He had a wonderful view of the backs of other triple-deckers with the exception of the corner where there was an auto body shop.

He sat outside off and on for a few hours thinking about Chloe, the psychiatrist, the dreams and work. He couldn't seem to shut off his brain and really relax. He played some video games and watched TV. The evening had come before he knew it so he watched a movie and fell asleep in front of the TV.

He was jostled awake by another odd dream in the wee hours of the morning and it took him a minute to collect himself and realize where he was. An info commercial for "the last frying pan you'll ever own" blared at him as bits and pieces of the dream came into focus.

He was in the hallway of some industrial building. There were words on the wall that he couldn't read. He saw a fire extinguisher attached to the wall with the word seguridad above it. He looked through a window to the manufacturing floor below and saw people working on some sort of machine. He had no idea what it was or what it meant.

After a few minutes, Perry got up, shut off the TV and went to his bed. He fell fast asleep and the rest of the night was uneventful. He woke up to more bits and pieces of the dream. He had entered a room that read zona segura. There was a laboratory with some electronic schematics on a table. He couldn't recall much more.

A text from David broke the silence.

Yo. WSP

Not much

U fine after Friday?

AFAIK

Wild time

IKR

Want to hang?

K

                                             Hoops?

Yah

                                         My place 1 hr

K

Perry knew David wouldn't let up and appreciated his friend's effort to keep him from being alone. He didn't want to stay in the apartment and dwell on everything so he readily agreed to go out.

The pair played a game of one on one and then more players came and they formed a game. More and more players came and it turned into an afternoon. They hit a fast-food restaurant on the way home and talked. Perry didn't bring up the latest dreams. After another hour or so, they each went home.

Monday was a standard work day for Perry. Nothing out of the ordinary except that he called the psychiatrist who had an opening two days later due to a cancellation. Perry took it despite his own anxiety because he promised David. The anxiety built for a solid day as he contemplated what would happen in the appointment. He figured it would be a lot of talking about his childhood, loved his mother and wanted to kill his father. You know, all that Freud stuff.

The appointment was Wednesday in the late afternoon so Perry left work early. It was only a few miles away in a small home off the main road that was surrounded by a strip mall and a car dealership. Clearly the owner refused to sell to developers.

Perry spent the first 20 minutes filling out all the paperwork for insurance and then made a sizable copay because his insurance was mediocre. He scanned the walls that had different paintings and one was an abstract rendering of the Starship Enterprise from Star Trek.

He sat there waiting for Dr. Lynch in a small waiting room.

When he appeared, he was not the picture he recalled from the website of him sitting at his desk. Instead, he opened the door and almost filled the entire door frame with his height. He wore no jacket and tie, just a pullover sweater with the collar of a button-down shirt emerging from the neck hole. He wore corduroy pants and brown loafers. He had disheveled white hair and wore wire rim glasses on his wrinkled face.

"Come in Perry," the doctor said. "I am Dr. Lynch."

Perry greeted him, walked over to the couch and laid down.

"Oh, I'd rather you sit up so we can speak face to face," said Dr. Lynch.

"Sorry," Perry said. "I just thought I was supposed to lay down."

"Maybe several appointments later," smiled Dr. Lynch, who realized Perry had never been to a psychiatrist before. "We're just going to talk for now so I can get to know you."

"Okay," said Perry, who was now sitting up on the leather couch.

"You comfortable? Would you like a water, Kombucha, coffee or cocaine?" asked the doctor.

"What?" exclaimed Perry.

"Just a joke," Dr. Lynch chuckled. "I wanted to make sure you were listening. My patients are always stunned when I say Kombucha."

Perry laughed. The joke had done the job as Perry's defenses had come down. Dr. Lynch had recognized the anxiety Perry exhibited and successfully made him comfortable.

The doctor scanned through some of the details of the paperwork that Perry had filled out online and in the waiting room.

"I see you've had some trauma in your life with your dad and now a girlfriend," he stated.

"Yeah. That's why I am here. Chloe's death is bothering me. My friend David came to you years ago and suggested that I should talk to you."

"Yes, indeed. You've been having dreams."

"Yeah. It's odd. I was jumping off a cliff in one and then in some building in another."

The doctor asked Perry to elaborate and he did, talking about the dreams for 10 minutes as the doctor wrote down notes. He only interjected a few times to get additional details.

"Did you have any dreams of this nature after your father died?" he asked.

Perry pulled himself off the back cushion of the couch and sat straight up. It was a thought that had not struck him before. His dad had died when he was 15 and he remembers being an emotional wreck, but never wondered if he had dreams.

"I'm not sure," Perry began. "I have always had dreams. I seldom remembered them like these dreams. I am reading signs in these dreams."

"What's the earliest dream you recall," asked Dr. Lynch.

Perry chuckled because he wasn't sure. He thought about it and amazingly recalled a dream when he was in his youth when his dad was still alive.

"A red truck," he exclaimed. "I remember a red truck going down the road. I must have been six. It was clear as day and I think that was the first dream in color I ever had."

The doctor wrote it down and looked back at Perry, who thought some more about other dreams.

"I remember being about 12 and having the same dream a few times," he said. "My dad and I were outside. He was doing some lawn work and I was just playing. I was wearing a light waterproof rain coat. I put my hands in the pockets and flipped the jacket over my lower back. It caused me to fly into the air. I remember looking down at my dad and calling to him but he didn't answer."

"Interesting," said Dr. Lynch.

"I can't believe I remembered that," said Perry. "What does it mean?"

"I don't know, but you do. We'll figure it out together."

Perry nodded his head and felt very comfortable with Dr. Lynch, who didn't offer much but listened very well.

"You don't recall any dreams after your father's death but Chloe's death has been the trigger now," the doctor stated.

Perry sat there processing the correlation the doctor pointed out and simply nodded.

"We're close to time and we are at a good stopping point," explained Dr. Lynch. "I'd like you to think about other dreams you have had at any time in your life that have happened more than once and any that seem odd to you. Write them down because it will provide insights for you and me."

The doctor stood up as did Perry, who shook the doctor's hand and thanked him. Perry went out and made another appointment with the assistant. He left with a lot to think about.

Perry went home and made dinner for himself that he ate while watching the local news. David texted him to see how the appointment went and Perry sent him two thumbs up emojis. The remainder of the evening was spent watching TV and reading a magazine.

He went to bed and wondered what dreams he would have that night. Would they be weird? Would they be the same dreams as before? Would it be about his childhood?

It was about three in the morning when Perry woke up in a cold sweat after yet another dream. This was different than before. He dreamed about his dad and his cousin Alan, but it was more about Alan's family. He recalls his dad, Alan's mom (his aunt), Alan's dad (his uncle) and Alan's wife but Alan was not there. His aunt was just shaking her head the whole time. They were high up in the sky. His dad pointed to the right and said Boston was in that direction. He then pointed to the left and said Buffalo was in that direction.

It was quite obvious to him that Alan wasn't there because he died. Perry's dad had come to tell this to him. Alan was very much alive so Perry took this as a warning. He jumped out of bed to call Alan but realized it was the early morning and he would sound nuts. He figured he'd wait until Saturday's annual family barbeque at Uncle Billy's to tell Alan.

Perry jumped out of bed to fire up his computer. He wondered where they were in the dream. Where were they that they could see Buffalo and Boston? Perry got a map of the United States and enlarged the northeast until Buffalo and Boston were in the frame. He took two rulers and held them to the screen to see what major city they would crisscross. New York City.

He took a deep breath and realized that his younger cousin Alan was going to die in New York City. He got overly emotional because Alan was going to start Grad School at Columbia in NYC that fall.

Perry got up and paced around the apartment and heard Samantha start walking around the apartment. He feared he woke her up again. She said she was a deep sleeper but why is she always up at the same time? He must be causing it. This was something he definitely jotted down to tell Dr. Lynch.

The next few days until the barbeque dragged for Perry who was chomping at the bit to talk to Alan. He struggled at work that Friday as the thought of what this dream meant just tore at him. He was not prepared for what happened next. His cell phone rang and it was the secretary from the doctor's office. Dr. Lynch had passed away the night before unexpectedly. The secretary said something about an undiagnosed heart problem.

"Just like Chloe," he thought.

Perry had nobody to confide in now. Perhaps he could talk to David. He thought about talking to his Uncle Billy but he didn't think that would be wise. He liked his uncle but wasn't sure he trusted him. There was something about him that he found unsettling but he couldn't identify.

Perry got through Friday struggling with the death of Chloe and now his doctor. He woke up early Saturday morning but had to wait until mid-afternoon to leave for the barbecue. Uncle Billy lived about an hour away just over the New Hampshire border. He had several acres that included a lot of woods.

He always joked that his uncle was a survivalist but that wasn't far from the truth. His uncle was former military like his dad, but wasn't a career man. He had quite a few guns at the house and had a lot of supplies. He assumed his uncle had a bunker somewhere on the property and hoped he was part of the lucky ones to be invited to it if anything happened.

He didn't know what to do with himself so he started cleaning his apartment. He swept the floor for the first time in weeks and then washed down the counters and the table. He realized it was nervous energy because it was not an easy subject to broach.

"Hi Alan. Good to see you again. Don't go to NYC or you're going to die," he thought.

He had to find a better way than that so he focused on a way to explain himself without coming off crazy all while scrubbing the stove and the sinks. It was good therapy to clean. He wasn't a neat freak but he felt better when the place was clean.

He finally left for the barbeque and stopped at the supermarket that he worked for to get his uncle's favorite light beer. On the ride up, he listened to his iPod that included Matchbox Twenty, 3 Doors Down, Black Eyed Peas and more. One particular Matchbox Twenty song spoke to him.

"But I'm not crazy, I'm just a little unwell. I know right now you can't tell, but stay awhile and maybe then you'll see a different side of me."

The invite said the gathering was 3 p.m. until you drop where you stand. Uncle Billy had a big house and took your keys and made you stay if you imbibed too many victuals. Perry was the first to arrive just a few minutes after 3 pm, greeting his aunt and uncle.

He feared he was projecting a nervous energy vibe that Uncle Billy would pick up on. His dad and uncle were both good reading people and it was probably because they had military training. It didn't hurt that Uncle Billy was a cop for about eight years until he got injured on the job and had to retire.

Perry kept an eye out for Alan as he talked to his uncle and a few other early guests. It was an hour into the barbeque and Alan had not arrived nor did his parents. He already asked his uncle about Alan and couldn't ask again.

The pool was sparkling right next to him and some of the children were already splashing around. Perry didn't think to bring his bathing suit but now wished he did.

Perry went and grabbed his fourth beer and his uncle took notice.

"You okay Perry?" he asked. "You're hitting the IPAs a little hard."

"Oh, yeah," said Perry. "I've never had this brand before. I tried it and really liked it."

"Some of those craft beers are really good," he responded. "Just remember I've got a bed for you here at the house if you have too many of them."

Perry shook his head and realized Uncle Billy had already picked up on the vibe. He realized he better slow down on the beers and just chill. Alan would arrive at some point and he needed to be cool about it.

It was close to 6 p.m. when the meats were ready. Uncle Billy made the standard fare of hot dogs, hamburgers, sausages, steak tips, chicken and brisket. This was on top of the various appetizers his aunt made as well as the various desserts and salads that the guests brought. It was a veritable feast that could serve a hundred people even though there was only about a third of that many people there.

Perry sat down at one of the tables with a plate of food and spied Alan coming in. He took a bite of his hot dog and then made a bee line to his cousin.

"Hi Alan. Good to see you. Can we talk?" he said, realizing he had completely gone off script.

Alan tried to come in and greet other people but Perry insisted, practically making a little scene.

"Can't it wait about a half hour man?" asked Alan. "I mean I haven't even come in yet."

Perry insisted and they went inside the basement of the house for some privacy. Uncle Billy noticed the incident and put a friend in charge of the grill. He stealthfully followed the two and listened as best he could.

Perry tells Alan, who stands there for a moment thinking his cousin has lost his mind. After a moment of silence, Alan walks away and Perry tries to follow. Uncle Billy intercepts Perry and puts his hand on his nephew's shoulder to stop him.

"Hold on Perry," said Uncle Billy. "What's going on with you today? The last time I saw you like this was when your dad died."

Perry looked up and realized that three people have now identified his behavior as related to his father's death.

"I don't want to talk about it," Perry began.

"Come on," his uncle started. "Tell your Uncle Billy what's up. I always told you I am your second father and would take care of you and look out for you."

Perry hems and haws a bit and is very fidgety. He doesn't make eye contact with his uncle and just looks around the room. His uncle puts his hands on each of Perry's shoulders and turns him so they are looking directly at each other.

"I'm not going to drop this son," Uncle Billy said. "Tell me the truth."

It took a moment but Perry felt the emotion well up inside of him and it just burst out of him in a crying fit. He tried to speak but heard himself just making gibberish. Uncle Billy pulled his nephew into his arms and held him for a few minutes until Perry collected himself.

"I'm good now," Perry said as he pulled away from his uncle, who motioned for Perry to sit on the day bed in the corner of the basement. Uncle Billy sat down next to him.

"Why was it so important to talk to Alan right away?" Uncle Billy asked.

Perry took a deep breath and began to explain.

"I had a dream that Alan was going to die in NYC," Perry said. "I have been having weird dreams that I am somewhere doing something. They seem so real."

Uncle Billy shakes his head and just listens as his nephew bares all that is troubling him. He barely says anything as Perry talks about his father's death, Chloe's death, his doctor's death and goes into detail about the dreams.

When his nephew finally stops, Uncle Billy offers some assurances of support and clasps his hands together. Perry has always looked up to his father and uncle and awaits his uncle's words, but was not prepared for what he was about to learn.

"I have something to tell you about your dad," Uncle Billy said. "I always knew this day would come. And the time seems to be now."

Perry's eyes widened as Uncle Billy told him about his dad's early years.

"Your father had dreams, similar to the dreams you explain," he said. "It began when he was much younger than you. It all started a few months after your dad and I attended a camp up here in New Hampshire. He was 14 and I was 11. Father McCall, the local priest at St. Joseph's where we went for mass, selected us both to go to this camp because we were poor.

"It was a fun place. We swam, played ball, board games and so much more. It was one of the happiest times of our childhood. But there were some mornings when we got shots and other mornings when we got pills. It took some time for me to realize this, but all the other kids there had a brother or sister with them. One sibling was a test subject and the other was the control group. Your dad was the test subject and I was the control group."

"The priest sent you there to be tested on?" Perry exclaimed. "Who was testing you?"

"I think it was the military," Uncle Billy said with a heavy sigh. "I think that's why your father and I both joined when we were older."

Perry was stunned, but continued to listen as Uncle Billy continued.

"The dreams were all over the place and your father couldn't make sense of them. Your grandparents didn't understand and passed off the dreams as nonsense. But I think your dad was having these dreams again that led him to commit suicide."

"Oh my God," Perry exclaimed. "Dad never mentioned any of this."

"Well, there's more," Uncle Billy said.

"More!" Perry yelled. "What else?"

"After the Vietnam war ended," Uncle Billy began, "Your father entered the military's Project Stargate in 1977."

"My dad was going to be an astronaut?" Perry interjected.

"Not exactly," said Uncle Billy. "It was a secret spy project started by the defense department. The CIA, NSA and other organizations were involved. They investigated the potential use of psychic phenomena for use by the military. The Nazis were doing this during World War 2. We caught wind that the Russians were experimenting with this in the early 1970s so we had to keep up.

"Project Stargate primarily involved remote viewing, which is the purported ability to psychically see events, sites or information from afar. Your father was one of 20 to 25 test subjects who showed an ability to do this. The project was terminated and declassified in 1995 after a report concluded that it was never useful in any intelligence operation. Information provided by the program was vague and included irrelevant and erroneous data. Well, that's what they said. I'm not so sure the project ended."

"I was born in 1995," Perry said. "Does that mean anything?"

"Your father thought so," said Uncle Billy. "Your name Perry is a shortened version of Peregrine that means traveler in Latin."

Perry buried his hand on his forehead and let out an audible gasp. Uncle Billy placed his hand on Perry's shoulder.

"Your father thought the military was still secretly using him or experimenting with him from a distance," Uncle Billy explained. "Hence, the crazy dreams that didn't make sense to him, but might have made sense to agents who were his handlers."

Perry just sat there with his mouth agape, trying to process all this information.

"Are my dreams now evidence that they are continuing these experiments with me?" Perry asked.

"Possibly," Uncle Billy said. "It may be a hereditary ability. Maybe they are tapping your psyche the way they did your dad's."

Perry let that sink in and wanted to scream. This was all too much for him on top of everything else.

"What can I do about this?" Perry demanded. "I'm not some damned guinea pig!"

"No, you're not," said Uncle Billy.

"Are you a remote viewer?" Perry asked.

"No," he said. "Your father explained the process of it, so we tried. I just don't have any ability to do it."

"But I do," Perry said. "So that dream of me on the island was remote viewing?"

Perry was upset of everything he had just learned about his dad and the fact that the military might be using him as a spy asset, but he was also a bit interested by the prospect that he could "travel" psychically to other locations.

"If I can remote view, could I use it to find who is doing this to me?" he asked

Uncle Billy raised an eyebrow at this prospect and thought it was a possibility.

"Stay here tonight," requested Uncle Billy. "We can talk more and try to figure something out."

The door to the basement burst open and Aunt Martha popped in.

"There you two are," she said. "What are you doing? You're missing the barbecue, You're neglecting our friends Bill."

"We're just talking things through," Uncle Billy said. "But we're done in here. Let's get back to the fun Perry."

Aunt Martha shook her head and walked out of the room followed by Perry and his uncle. The rest of the afternoon was uneventful. The festivities wound down in the early evening and many people left. But there were a few stragglers around the fire pit drinking beers and telling stories. By 11 pm, everyone had left. Perry stayed behind as his uncle requested. Aunt Martha prepared a guest room for her nephew.

After she left, Uncle Billy came in with a piece of paper.

"Let's see how well you can remote view," he said as he closed the door.

"I'm really tired and perhaps a bit drunk," said Perry.

"That's the best time," Uncle Billy explained. "You will sleep deeper and the alcohol will act like some of the drugs they gave your dad to open the mind."

Perry went along because he knew his uncle was trying to help him.

"Lay down and look at these numbers on this piece of paper," Uncle Billy said.

"What are these numbers?" Perry asked.

"Coordinates," Uncle Billy said. "Longitude and Latitude."

Perry looked at the numbers and had no idea what they meant, but it occurred to him the Illinois phone number were coordinates. He stared at them for several minutes and started to get drowsy. He heard his uncle telling him to relax. Soon enough, he drifted off to a hypnotic state where he was not quite asleep and not quite awake. Uncle Billy noticed the eyes under his nephew's eyelids were moving quickly. Perry had fallen into rapid eye movement, known as REM, that is a sign of dreaming.

"Where are you right now?" Uncle Billy asked.

"I'm in the woods," said Perry.

"Ok, keep going into the woods and find the coordinates," Uncle Billy said in a soft, comforting voice.

"I see something; I see a bunch of rocks."

"Can you describe them?"

"Some are big. Others are small. There some standing upright. There's one that is flat and sits on top of other rocks. There is a line around all four sides of the flat rock. It's like a … a … gutter. It's about a half-inch deep and one of the lines runs off the flat rock to a basin below it."

"What else do you see?"

"The sun is rising. It looks like it is balancing on a rock a hundred feet away. It's casting a shadow on another rock next to me."

"Good. … Good. Anything else?"

"There's a cave. It's a small cave. I am inside. It opens up a bit and there is an opening in the top of it and then sunlight is starting to shine through it."

"Excellent. Come back to the bedroom and slowly wake up."

"Wait. I see people. They are natives. It's a tribe. They are coming into the cave."

"Do they know you are there?"

"I don't know. Wait. They do. They are talking to me."

"What are they saying?"

"A prayer perhaps. I'm not sure."

"Come back Perry. Come back to the bedroom."

Within a few seconds, Perry opened his eyes and his uncle's face came into view.

"Oh my God; What was that?" he exclaimed. "Where was I? Where did you send me? Who were those people?"

Uncle Billy was in awe of his nephew's ability and a little surprised that Perry enjoyed the adventure. But his brother did too at first before it all turned sour.

"The coordinates I gave you were not too far away," Uncle Billy explained. "The location was America's Stonehenge in Salem, New Hampshire. It's an archaeological site consisting of a number of large rocks and stone structures scattered around roughly 30 acres. You described it very well. But who were the people?"

"They were a tribe," Perry said. "They were Native Americans and they knew I was there."

"It's disputed who built the site. Some say Native Americans but others say it was Europeans who came here in the 1600s," explained Uncle Billy. "You not only traveled to the site. But you seem to have traveled back in time."

Perry's eyes were as wide as an owl as he processed everything that had just happened.

"What does it all mean?" Perry asked.

"It means your ability is far greater than your dad's," Uncle Billy said. "It's 2 am so get some sleep and we'll talk tomorrow."

"We've been doing this for two hours?" Perry realized.

Uncle Billy stood up and walked to the door.

"Get some rest," he began. "I've got a plan to try and figure out who is doing this to you and to stop it. We'll try it tomorrow."

The next morning arrived and Perry woke up to the smell of breakfast wafting down the hall. Auntie Martha had made eggs, bacon, hash browns and sausage. Perry got dressed and followed his nose to the kitchen.

"Welcome sleepy head," said Aunt Martha, causing Perry to smile.

"This looks fantastic; thank you," Perry said.

"A big breakfast just in case you didn't have enough to eat yesterday," replied Aunt Martha.

"I've got a plan to try and figure this out," Uncle Billy said. "We'll try in the afternoon after you have had more time to rest."

Perry gave his uncle the "don't talk about this in front of Auntie Martha" look that she picked up on.

"I know everything honey," Aunt Martha said.

"You told her?" Perry yelled at Uncle Billy.

"Your father told her," Uncle Billy began. "He told both of us everything. He came up often to discuss everything that was going on."

"It's okay sweetie," Aunt Martha said in her motherly way. "We are going to help you."

After they finished breakfast, they began the process of cleaning up. Perry helped and then sat down on the deck with one of those IPAs he discovered that weekend. He was working on his second IPA when his aunt and uncle came over and sat down.

"I am thinking that the woman who moved upstairs from you is tied to this," Uncle Billy mused. "I took the liberty of getting the coordinates for your building so you can remotely get into her apartment."

"That will be intense," Perry said.

"I am going to have you go to your apartment first," Uncle Billy explained. "We don't want her to see you so we're going to get her out of the house."

"Understood," Perry said.

The three went to the guest bedroom and Perry laid down. Uncle Billy called Samantha's number and made up some story to get her out of the house. They started the process after 20 minutes.

Perry focused on the coordinates and seemed to get there rather quickly. He was in his own apartment at the front door. He walked to the center of the living room and listened for her. He heard nothing and said that to his uncle. He also reported that he didn't see her car so the ruse Uncle Billy staged worked.

"Okay now go to her apartment," Uncle Billy said.

Perry just ascended upwards instead of taking the stairs. He was in her living room and noticed a whole bunch of computers, a table with a lot of chemistry apparatus and a log book with Perry Project on it. There was also a white erase board with details about him, his father and uncle Billy. He reported this all to his uncle.

Perry then heard some commotion.

"I think she's home," he reported.

"Okay," Uncle Billy said. "Go back to your apartment."

Perry focused and was back in his apartment. At the other end of the room was Samantha standing on a ladder inserting an electronic device into the smoke alarm. She was looking right at him.

"I found Samantha," Perry said. "She saw me."

"Come back right away," Uncle Billy said.

And just like that Perry was back in the bedroom at the aunt and uncle's home.

"We don't have much time," Uncle Billy said. "We have to go to your apartment and get evidence. Maybe confront her."

"Wait!" Perry exclaimed. "Your name was on a white board. Why?'

"Because they tested your dad. They tried it on me but I was not capable," he explained.

"You telling me the truth?" Perry demanded. "Are you part of this? The both of you?"

"Whoa! Hold on Perry," Uncle Billy cautioned. "This is exactly what happened to your dad. The remote viewing started blurring the line of reality and he got paranoid."

"We are on your side honey," said Aunt Martha.

"I'm getting a gun and then we can go," Uncle Billy said. "You want a gun?"

"What? No!" said Perry.

Within a few minutes, Uncle Billy and Perry were on the road racing to get to Perry's apartment. They got there in less than an hour. When they arrived, Samantha's car was gone. They went up the stairs to her apartment and tried the door but it was locked.

Uncle Billy pulled out a few tools from his pocket and picked the lock.

"You're a former cop," Perry said. "That's illegal."

"It's only breaking and entering if you get caught," Uncle Billy said.

He drew his gun and motioned for Perry to stand off to the side. Uncle Billy burst through the door and went through the apartment but nobody was there.

"It's clear," he yelled and summoned Perry into the apartment.

Perry looked around and the computers, chemistry apparatus, white board log book and everything else was gone.

"She saw you and aborted the mission," Uncle Billy said. "They packed up and split in the time it took us to get here."

"That was only 45 minutes." Perry asked. "How'd they do it so fast?"

"They are very good at what they do," Uncle Billy explained.

"Now what?" Perry asked.

"We search for evidence here and in your place but we won't find anything," Uncle Billy explained. "We have to wait until they start with you again."

"It's not over then?" Perry questioned.

"Only temporarily," Uncle Billy explained.

The pair looked around Samantha's apartment as well as Perry's but found nothing.

Meanwhile, a four-star general walked into a conference room with gray walls in an industrial building somewhere in the country. There were several people sitting at the conference room and they all stood up when the general entered.

"Be seated," he said. "We are going to temporarily shut down this mission with the Perry boy. We'll get back to it sometime in the future because he was one of our best assets as was his father. I want to congratulate Agents Hermann and Chester for a job well done. Because of the two of you and your fine work, we got some very good intel on what the Cubans are doing at their secret lab in Cuba. Do you have anything else to report?"

"I want to apologize again for blowing the mission sir," said Agent Hermann. "I didn't anticipate he would figure out what was going on and would remote view into his apartment and mine."

"That's not on you," the general said. "That's on Bill and Martha. They clearly helped their nephew. They still hold a grudge after the death of Bill's brother."

"Should we do something about Bill sir?" asked Agent Chester. "If he's getting in the way, we could eliminate him like we did Dr. Lynch."

"Lynch was a liability because of his hypnosis therapy so we had to go to protect the project. But I don't think that would be wise to eliminate Bill," said the general. "We might need him and his wife because we want to try and work with Perry in the future."

"The kid has already lost his dad," he continued, "and, technically, Agent Hermann, who posed as his girlfriend Chloe and is now presumed dead by Perry. If he lost his uncle and aunt, there's no telling what he would do now that he has discovered this ability. Nothing is more dangerous than a man who can remote view with nothing to lose."

ABOUT THE AUTHOR

GIOVANNI ALABISO is the owner of Salem Historical Tours and Haunted Footsteps Ghost Tour that gives walking tours about the history and paranormal in Salem, Massachusetts, where the infamous 1692 Witchcraft Trials occurred. He also owns Witch City Gift Shop that sells souvenirs and unique gifts.

He is a former sports/news journalist having worked for major metropolitan newspapers in Boston as well as daily newspapers in Greater Boston.

He is a retired CPA having worked for a top national accounting firm. He also worked as a controller at a few private companies, conducted audits for the state of Massachusetts and did some forensic accounting for the FBI.

He is also an actor, comedian and producer. He did standup and improv comedy for about 15 years in New England and NYC. He has acted in several independent movies and been featured in a myriad of feature films, sometimes with lines and sometimes not. He was also in a play called Fishnet Networks.net that ran in Boston's Theatre district for three years. He has also produced a few movies of his own as well as plays and comedy shows.

Giovanni is also a historian. He has researched and written about the Salem Witchcraft Hysteria for 15 years. Most of his presentations have been on walking tours, but he also has done presentations at conferences, local organizations and via zoom. And being in Salem, he also regales visitors to the city with stories of ghosts and the paranomal.

He was also the host of an internet talk show called Salem History & Beyond that ran for two years during covid and featured many experts and authors in the field of witchcraft.

And now he adds "Published Author" to the list.

His website is GiovanniAlabiso.com and you can find his company at SalemHistoricalTours.com

www.ingramcontent.com/pod-product-compliance
Lightning Source LLC
Chambersburg PA
CBHW020038280925
33249CB00003B/4